ENTER THE GUARDIANS:

KYL

BOOK ONE

W. Shane Wilson

Distributed through LULU.com
First printing: 2009
Book Printed in America (via digital printer)
ISBN: 978-0-578-00797-7

All characters in this book are fictitious; any resemblance to an actual person is living or dead is coincidental.

THIS BOOK IS DEDICATED TO ALL THE FIGHTERS, MARTIAL ARTIST AND SOLDIERS OUT THERE YOUNG AND ELDER WHO RISK IT ALL TO PROTECT AND SERVE THE ONES THEY LOVED. GOOD HUNTING.

TO PASTOR MIKE (GOODE) FOR ALL THE SOULS AND LIVES YOU TOUCHED THANKS YOU AND GOD BLESS OCT 1 1946   to   JAN 8 2009

CHAPTERS

Have you ever wondered what it would be like to have a real alien race descend on the earth? Well, it has finally happened one cold winter day. It was late November and the sun had not shown its face in three days, not a single ray. Smoke rose from the chimney in the cabin tucked into the trees. Within the cabin was a solitary figure, Jillian. She was once a model; she is only 27 years old now. She still gets offers to model and act, her beauty and elegance is so natural and easy that she never wore makeup, she did not need it. She moved out to nowhere to be left in peace. She gave it all up because her friend and fellow super model was murdered by a crazed fan, and the law did nothing, because the Fan was well placed.

The winding sound of a well tuned motor whispered over the snow fields, as a another dark figure ripped thru the night toward Jillian. The snow fell and the wind blew, and nothing kept the figure from reaching his target. Jillian was drawing her evening boiling hot bath and did not hear the figure approach. The robe fell to the floor as Jillian slipped her highly coveted body into the steaming water.

The stranger watched Jillian remove her clothing, and enjoyed the moment as she walked around nude prior to slipping into the water. Quietly, the figure entered the cabin and even more soundlessly, removed their outerwear and boots. Light glinted off the blade of a razor in the cabins half light. The figure stopped by the fire and added a log. Slipping into the bathroom blade in hand, they approached Jillian. She was lying back with her breast barely visible under the hot soapy water. Her throat was exposed and her eyes were closed. The stranger smiled then put the knife to Jillian's throat, she gasped in surprise.

"Do you know how hard these things are to come by, well, no of course not. Jill asks and Brig gets. I am half froze Jilly, you could at-least invite me into your hot tub" Brig said softly into Jillian's ear?

"You scared the hell out of me Brig" Jillian said standing up in the tub, "Well off with those cloths, if you want to get in". She giggled. "Besides I need the knife for my art project, you wanted me to be happy right". She smiled and melted his heart.

The one person in the whole world that Jillian could not, would not be without was the strange boy she meet as a 5 year old. He moved to her town right next to her back then. He could even as a small child do anything, figure out anything. He was not a big guy, he was no male model. He was a real man, her real man. She loved him since she was five. The local bully pushed her down and took her new bike away, the one she got for her 5th birthday. Before, she even began to cry the new little boy from next door; he was across the yard in a rush; he never spoke, tackled the bully to the ground. Before the bully could get to his feet, the smaller boy had him by his hair throttling him. Even the parents stood by and gawked as a tiny boy of five mercilessly punish a giant eight year old.

The bully screamed "I AM SORRY JILLIAN, I GIVE UP"!

The small boy let him go and walked over to the bike and pushed it back to Jillian. He pulled off his tee shirt and wiped the blood off her handlebars that dripped from his tore up knuckles. Jillian looked into his wee little face and knew she would love this boy her whole life. She was right. She bandaged his busted hands herself, not wanting anyone to touch her hero. Brig was her first and only love; and her first kiss, dance, boyfriend and lover.

Jillian was the most beautiful child in her town. Then she grew up the most popular gorgeous girl in her town, then the county, the state, the planet.

Strange, through it all Brig was there quietly supporting her, caring for her, loving her. He acted like she was free to leave him behind and move on to better things, but she could not. He was the BEST thing there was. He re-earned that title everyday by his action toward Jillian. Jillian was always sought after. She had many men and women offer her sex, money, anything, all she wanted she found in this man, her champion, her heart, her life. So lucky for her that he loved her more than his own next heart beat.

The bath was just what the doc ordered, it did not relax Brig, In fact he attacked Jillian like a hungry bear. He always did. His love and desire for her was never quenched or satisfied. She moan in a warm splashing paradise as Brig made her relive and remember why she never wanted to be apart from him. Covered in soap, and laughing like kids, they enjoyed the best life could bring...each other. Brig rinse them off, and carried Jillian to the quilt in front of the fire, where they lay, nuzzling and snuggling the rest of the night away. Jillian's last thought prior to falling to sleep was how perfect life was once Brig was part of it.

This would be the last great week of her life, and Brig would be marked as a killer and hunted very soon.

CHAPTER ONE: TERRAFERMA

The sounds in space that you can hear, are not like the ones you hear planet side. They are distorted and eerie. The most common is the sound of twisting metal or something that resembles a bulkhead coming apart. I am sure that Naval personal could identify with this noise. However, none of them have ever traveled interstellar I would bet. The old cliché about a great alien craft crashing and the evil or friendly aliens coming out; has no place in this tale. The ship that is orbiting the Earth is a millennia ahead of anything on our planet, maybe even more in technology. The Kylr (Kel R) are a slate blue bald headed humanoid race. The females of their race look like human women, but the all have long grey, white or silver hair, and very fit sexy figures. Both male and females of the Kylr are very intelligent and hard working.

They are a well oiled machine in all things, work, play, sex. Very utilitarian, fun is not a concept they understand. Oh, but they will, they will learn a great deal from this exploration.

The last calm morning of Brig's life was also the most sweet. Jillian woke up Brig gently, by kissing her way up from his toes, he began to giggle even before he was actually awake. She was hiding under the covers and so he pulled them over his head to join her. It was late morning when they finally pulled themselves apart and had something to eat. It is important to understand how deeply they love each other, for this story and it's strange circumstances to be fully felt as far as the gravity goes. There will be great self sacrifices made in the name of love, with no regrets; and only joy at the result.

The sound of wood chopping could be heard echoing through the snow blanketed topography. Jillian was in the cabin washing some clothes and doing general chores, yes, she is a handy girl to have around. She and Brig had always been self sufficient; they depended on no one when they could do it for themselves. Beside, work kept them fit and flexible for other activities. Brig was so intent on his work he did not notice three men steal up to the cabin. Jillian was singing a happy song, she usually did, and she had a beautiful voice to boot, so it was nice to hear.

The first of the men pulled a syringe from his pocket and made his way toward Jillian from behind. The second secure the back door with a 9MM in his hand. The third watched the front door also with a pistol at the ready. They were most likely professional kidnappers. If they had decided to just do their job, it might have went off without a hitch. However, Jillian pulled of the old tee shirt she was wearing and tossed it In to the wash, so she was standing there naked. The man stood transfixed on the spot. Then he turned to his partners and said " let's play with her first". These were the last words of his life. Jillian heard him and hit him as hard as she could in the head with a steam iron. He hit the floor dead. Jillian screamed.

The man with the 9MM shot Jillian in the chest. Brig burst through a window like a wild animal. Bullets sprayed the room. The man by the front door ran forward firing his pistol at Brig. Two bullets found purchase in Brig's body. Even though they hit home, they did not stop the fire poker from impaling the luckless killer. The man gagged as he looked down at the metal protruding from his throat, he looked at Brig in surprise, smiled and fell stoned dead. Jillian was laying on the floor with the last man standing over her; she was clearly bleeding to death. The man looked up at Brig swiftly covering the blood drenched floor and raised his Glock and riddled Brig with it. To the man's utter horror, it did not slow Brig even a step. Brig took the mans head nearly off with the hatch in his hand.

The blood was running out Brig mouth like a fountain, he paid no heed to it. He grabbed a roll of duct tape and wipe the blood from Jillian's breasts and taped the bullet hole shut, he pulled her forward and did the same to her back. He wrapped her in a heavy winter coat and carried her to the snowmobile. But decide to take the killers Land Rover instead. Brig is a country boy and can 4wheel with the best of them. He was setting the land speed record for snow when the car began to sputter. It was out of gas. Brig cursed himself for not checking, how stupid to let this happen and Jilly is dying!

Brig had blood coming from his mouth nosed and eyes. Tears of blood ran down his face. When the car stopped, Brig did not. He yanked off his coat and wrapped it also around Jillian, even blood soaked it was more heat for her, and the cold would make his system slow down long enough to get Jillian to the trade post before he died.

Can you imagine the scene? The Kylr were watching the planet when Jar and Kerra brought attention to Brig and Jillian's plight. The aliens watched with patience and wonder. It was obvious the male was in worse condition, and his life was hanging by the meager breath. Yet, he neither slowed down or showed any sign of this. The girl was bleeding and unconscious, but likely would live with care, this was not the case with the male, he was, how do humans say, his chips were cashed. His effort and valor touched Jar as a fellow warrior. Jar was becoming uncomfortable watching a brave man die.

"He is to be saved" Jar said, it was not a question, it was a fact.

Knee deep in the snow, moving at a fevered pace, roughly a mile from the post, Jillian coughed up blood. She opened her eyes. The sight of Brig made her heart suddenly stop. He was a walking corpse. He looked into her eyes but did not stop or faultier. He was beyond talking, all his strength was to be used to save his love. No matter what he would not fail, no matter what! Jillian noticed that blood was not coming out of the hole is Brig's chest, she knew this was not a good thing, but she was so weak she could not even move. Finally the post was in sight. However, Brig was done for. He did not drop Jillian, not even in death. He simple gently went to his knees and laid her on the snow. He was crying again.

"I am sorry, I love you" he whispered, then he threw back his head and scream in anguish so loud snow fell from the trees for miles.

Jillian used what strength she had left and placed her fingers on his face, she was also crying.

"You should have saved yourself, I don't want to live in a world that you not in. I love you don't leave me Brigand Sawyer, you have been my life since we were five years old, I can't be without you" Jillian choked out between tears.

"No, you Must live... for me" Brig whispered. Jillian slipped into a coma, and he died at that moment.

CHAPTER 2: GAUNTLET

In the cold of space you would think that nothing else exists but the cold dead vacuum. The Kylr crew was busy cloaking the craft while they did their work. The Kylr have been called meddlers by some of the other great races, the Kylr did not care about their opinions, they had taken to protecting the lesser races from the great races. Some who were not even slightly friendly, some were meat eaters and thought of Earth as a game refuge. Disgusting! Nonetheless, Jar who was special even among his own people; had taken the Earth case to the high council and demanded to privilege of protecting the humans, until they could protect themselves.

Brig lay on a silver metallic table; it was warm to the touch and seemed to ripple like water after a stone is tossed in, when the slightest movement was made. Brig had died a hero's death, protecting and caring for the one he cherished in life. Jar felt a kinship with this small human. He wanted to speak with him; and learn of the planet, and of Brig, but this was not the time.

On a separate table structure across the room Jillian lay nude as a goddess with silver hair use unfamiliar instruments on her. Brig opened his eyes, they hurts so bad he closed them again and remembered it all. With a sudden burst of power, yes power not energy, he opened his eyes and tried to sit up. He could not. So he turned his head to look at where his true love was. She seemed dead to him, except her breast where rising and falling gently. She was breathing softly. The female who was looking after Jillian was soft blue in color and had long silver hair and was totally naked as well. She turned and regarded Brig, smiled, then returned to her work. She was the second most beautiful women Brig had ever seen, next to Jillian. Her body and face were perfect in everyway.

"She is well Hero, she rests now. The damage to her heart was much worse than I thought to begin with. Your medicine would not have been able to save her. It would have been a shame after you spent your life to save hers." Said the alien girl. "What would you give me to spare her the horror of a scarred heart and body, she is very lovely"?

"I would give you anything you want to save her, make her well and you can name your price" Brig said.

"Done hero, it is a bargain. I am Kerra" said the blue girl.

She returned her full attention to Jillian.

A frightened girl opens her eyes and her hands went straight to her breasts, where she was shot a close range. She cannot find an injury although she is very sore and weak. Jillian began to cry as she remembered what her salvation cost. She was screaming in anguish, she had never felt such true misery and despair. Suddenly, there were strong hands on hers, she was drain out of her misery by curiosity. there was a soft blue women of incredible looks both her face and body with magnificent. The blue girl pulled firmly on her hands drawing Jillian off the bed she was on. Jillian was suddenly aware this was not a normal structure and this girl was not a normal girl.

They walked down hallways of smooth metal, entered a chamber with an octagonal window, Jillian slowed to look out and froze where she stood. What she saw was North America below her, her home. The blue girl smiled put her arm warmly around her. For the first time Jillian looked at her. She was not nude as Jillian thought but wore a garment that was the same color as her skin; she was well muscled and still exceptionally gorgeous and desirable.

"Come" said the blue girl.

Jillian had to be caught, her knees buckled when she was lead into where Brig lay dead on a metal slab. She began to cry so hard that she was inconsolable. A blue man with no hair but a powerful body picked Jillian up like a child and placed her next to Brig on the metal slab. Jillian put her head on his chest and cried herself into exhaustion.

She was sleeping so soundly and having the most wonderful dream of Brig and his body pressed to hers. She opened her eyes and Brig was looking at her, he had tiny pearls a moisture in his eyes. Jillian crawled on top of him and smothered him in kisses. She cried and laughed at the same time. Finally she sat up on his stomach and looked at him hard.

"This is only a dream, I saw you dead Brig, I am still asleep" Jillian said solemnly.

Brig pinched her hard on her nipple. She jumped. He sat up and kissed her where he pinched, rather lovingly. Her breath caught in her throat. "If we are dreaming I don't ever want to wake up Jilly" Brig said.

Jar and Kerra left Jillian to enjoy her lover once more in privacy, something that the Kylr did not care about. Jar sealed the chamber. Hours later Brig had cuddled Jillian to sleep once again.

The Kylr as a race are very rigid in their way of doing most things, Kerra is not hampered by this however. She is very different from her race on the whole. She is far above all the females of her race and most of the males mentally except for the Guardsmen, who are elite specimens in everyway. Kerra liked physical pleasure and loved Jar as much as any Kylr knows how. Kerra is the Brightest medical mind of her race, which makes her the greatest doctor in the known universe. She is the one who perfected the G-jen; although she did not create them. The G-jen is the jewel gauntlet the guardsmen wear. It gives them a terrible power, complete healing (Kerra's doing) and a double edge blade... immortality. Only the Kylr know this though, it is a secret. All others of the great races are held semi at bay from all out war by the Kylr guardians, whom are unbeatable for all purposes. They know this because for generations they tried everything to kill or beat them. All of their efforts failed them. Or so they thought, only Kerra and Jar know the truth of how close they finally came to breaking the Guardians power.

The Captain of the ship was not a guardsmen, but
he was a season officer and knew his job and vessel
well. He also knew that despite appearances Jar was
the real authority on this ship. He was Jar's oldest friend and
knew Jar would not assert his power unless he must. Saving the
Human couple was the first time in a long while that Jar had
gave an order. This made the Captain a bit at unease. Although
he was not a xenophobe, He was a Kylr and felt superior to all
races that were not. Jar who is not just a Guardian or Guardsmen
if you like, he was the absolute commander of all the armed force
and Guardians of the Kylr. He earned the right by trial by combat.
He had beaten all of the other guardians by himself without
seriously injuring any of them. The battle was held on a dead
planet because Jar refused to involve innocents in a private
matter.

When the 4 day battle came to an end; Jar was still standing
and all the Guardians kneeled and swore an oath to serve him as
leader until he steps down or is finally killed in combat. That was
200 years ago and Jar is no longer challenge for leadership. It is
said that Jar is the most deserving leader in all the great races;
he is respected not only for his strength but for his stewardship
and statesmanship as well. He is not known to make poor
choices however, some are not popular. Jar does not care about
his image, he cares about people and what is right to him. He is a
brave and true friend, if he is your friend; then he would crawl
into a supernova to save you from harm, with no thought for
himself. That, is what bothers the captain, Jar sees in the human
that very thing.

There was never more than one guardian on a ship or mission at
one time, unless there is war. Moreover, one guardian is usually
more than a match for anything. Only once in history had a
guardian turn against his peers, it was a terrible time. Jar himself
had to be summoned to deal with it. The guardian that went mad
was Jar's friend and he was nearly as powerful as Jar, thus he
was not about to let himself be defeated or captured. By the way,
a guardian can not be contained, so they must be destroyed,
which only possible if you can isolate the G-jen from the wearer,
if this is done the wearer dies a horrible painful death. Only one

soul knows how to do that so far and it is Jar. He is unwilling to ever explain this to anyone, even Kerra who often was his bed mate.

In the comfort of Jillian's arms Brig opened his eyes. He was woken by a strange sensation in his left forearm. It raised his arm to find it bandaged. Brig could not remember injuring his arm so he began to unwrap it. A strong but gentle hand covered his. He looked up into a blue face that had a single finger before its mouth. Brig was being summoned out of the chamber, so he followed. Once they were out of and away from the chamber the blue man finally spoke.

"Your female is very pleasant to look upon" said the blue dude.

"Yes, she certain is, nice to touch as well. The blue girl who was with you earlier is pretty hot too" Brig said, with a smile.

"Indeed, Kerra is most enjoyable, she is unique even among my race" The blue man told him. "The bandage on your arm is not to cover a wound, but to keep you from killing yourself or you female by accident".

"What"?

"Remove the bandage young man and look under it carefully at what is below, but I caution you not to touch it over much" The blue man said.

The bandage lay on the floor right where Brig dropped it. On Brigs left forearm was a beautifully crafted gauntlet with a great gem inlaid in the middle. It seemed to waver as you looked at it, like a 3D movie. Brig did not know what to think. He reached across with his right hand and was stopped by the blue man. Brig was about to snap at him, but just noticed that the blue man had an even more ornate gauntlet on his left forearm. So, Brig just relaxed.

"The G-jen is a weapon of unparalleled power, it is ancient and it is not to be taken for granted, or toyed with. If it comes away from your body you die a horrible death. It causes intense enough pain that you could die when it is placed on your arm, lucky for you that you were already dead when I placed it on you arm" Said the Blue man " I am Jar, your teacher and master for the time being".

"Dead...I really was dead" Brig said "Hey why did you put this on my arm"?

"Your world needs you, and so does the female" Jar said.

"My World" ask Brig?

"I will explain that to you later, for now I must teach you the rudimentary use of the G-jen, so that you are safe to be left alone" Jar began "There are other things I must explain that are vital; but they can wait until you can control the G-jen on a safe level" Jar finished.

Brig looked as though he wanted to speak, and then thought better of it and nodded his head for Jar to continue, which he of-course did.

"Strong emotions, are focused in the gem of the G-jen and channeled into useful powers" Jar explained.

"What kind of powers, how does it do that, how does it know" Asked Brig?

"Anger can product a beam of pure heat from your hands. Concern can be used to help heal others. Hate kills you and them, avoid hate" Jar told him. "You need to learn calmness clarity, serenity; these things are the base of our power. Your mind is the best weapon of all, use it. Strong emotions can be extremely useful when the time is right but they hamper you the rest of the time".

"What about joy and love, what will that bring" Brig asked?

"Happiness" Jar smiled.

The rest of the day or night Brig could not tell was spent in a room or part of the ship that opened into space but had a force shield that kept the atmosphere in and space out. Brig learned to gather his body heat and focus it. In the beginning all Brig could muster was small pops like a firework. By the time Jar called a halt to this session of his training, Brig could shatter the old pieces of the Apollo rocket bits left in orbit by NASA. Jar seemed to be pleased with Brig's progress. The last thing Jar taught him was to feel the power within the G-jen and calm or suppress it to a minimal level and keep it there. Basically control the power; do not let it control you ever. Brig was the first person Jar ever trained that could do it with almost no effort. Jar looked at him closely often Brig wondered why but did not ask.

Jillian woke to Kerra rubbing a sweet smelling liquid on her chest. Her first instinct was to repel her away, but she did not. Kerra was gently massaging her all over her upper body. It felt good. Kerra rolled Jillian on her side with a deft movement and massage her upper back, this also felt really good.

"I fixed the damage to your heart and lungs from the bones of your sternum exploding in there, but you seem to have a good deal of Myofacial pain, or at the least sub-sternal discomfort. This liquid is of my own creation; it will aid healing and relieve persistent pain." Kerra explained. "You thought I was in here to dabble with you, did you not" Kerra giggled like a naughty girl.

"Well, that did cross my mind Kerra, you are kind of a Manx if you know what I mean" Jillian said.

"True. We are not like you humans, we tend to suppress our feelings and emotions, I, howver, do not, I embrace them. You and Brig interest me greatly Jillian of earth. You are unique even for your people. Both of you are willing to make the ultimate sacrifice for the other, not just once but as many times as needed, and damn the personal cost." Kerra told her while running her hand across Jillian's cheek, "You are a true beauty, both in body and spirit".

"Thanks, I think. You seem to have the run of this place;
who are you to these people, and who are you to the blue man
who the others shy away from" Jillian asked while she reached
out and took Kerra's hand in hers?

"I am...(LOL) I am the greatest medical mind in the entire known
universe, I am a doctor. The best there is anywhere, this is not a
brag, it is a truth. I am also Jar's, the blue man you spoke of,
friend and often bed mate. Our people do not join like humans"
Kerra said.

"You mean your sex is different" Jillian whispered?

"(HAHAHAH), No child! We couple that same way, our
bodies are that same as yours pretty much, see for
 yourself" Kerra removed her sheer body suit".

    Jillian blushed which surprised her because she is
a model and has been around naked people her entire
life. It was different with Kerra she had a hungry aura to her that
you could feel, it was in the way she touched you, like she loved
and cherished the sensation of you. It made Jillian uncomfortable
and interested in the same moment. Kerra was blue and as tall
as Jillian. They looked at one another for a while. Jillian could
see no physical difference except skin color. Kerra took Jillian's
hand and placed it between her breasts. Jillian was going to pull
away but stopped and brought her other hand up under Kerra's
right rib cage below her breast and she gasped. No she wasn't
coping a feel, Kerra had two hearts beating in her perfect body.

"Yes, I have two hearts. It is why my race is so fit. Our
organs are very strong and efficient, except for reproduction
which is not very good among us" Kerra offered.

"What else is different anatomically about your people?" Jillian
asked.

"Well we have no sense of modesty, if we want we are free go bare or use garments. Also, we have no concept of marriage, we couple with anyone we want freely; since we are immune to disease, we need fear it not. More to the point; births are not as common as they once were, so if we are with child, we usually retain that lover to encourage more births in the future. Yet we may continue to have all the relationships we desire openly." Kerra told Jillian softly.

"I have only ever known Brig's touch, I desire no other." Said Jillian.

"Is that so, well that is your choice and it is to be respected at all times. We may be an open people; but personal freedoms are sacred to us, that is why The Guardians were founded." Kerra replied. "That is a topic for another time".

"So you and that Blue guy together" Jillian said "Does that give you a high position in life"?

"NO, I am chief medical officer for the Kylr, I am at the top already. Jar gives me pleasure, and he is my mental equal, I know I don't act like a scholar but I am. I have a lot of energy so I study, research and use my body for pleasure daily. Would you be angry if I bed your human friend"?

Jillian just looked at her for a long moment. "No, he is free to do as he pleases, but I doubt you could get his permission, he is a singular soul, very ...perfect. I love him with my entire being, and if he wants to be with you that will not change how I feel for him."

"Actually, when I was restoring you he gave his word to grant me anything I wanted. I also want you to help me with him, he could not refuse me if you asked him, we could share him together, you are also highly desirable." Kerra said "I would enjoy you if I could as well."

"I am flattered, but I have never...I just don't know." Jillian said.

"I really want to see if I could have a baby with him, if I was able: then it would also help to protect your world" Kerra told Jillian. "More important to me, it would help my race continue, I also wish for you to have his baby Jillian, he is a guardian now, his DNA is perfect, it would make a superior baby with both of us. I can offer your off-spring an unmatched education and you a life of adventure. Please help me" Kerra was practically was pleading.

Jillian held Kerra's hand and looked at the chamber door which just opened. Brig walked in and sat on their bed, kiss Jillian on the lips softly. Jar walked around to Kerra and squeezed her shoulders lightly. They were obviously very close, in an alien way.

"Did you ask her; He was told some things, but not of this?" Jar asked Kerra.

"She has been asked and shown that we are compatible, but she is reluctant being a human" Kerra said.

"NO DOUBT YOUR EXPLANATION" Jar snapped and turned to Jillian. He reached out and Brig stopped his hand eyes blazing. "No, no, calm yourself Brig, I was not going to hurt her or anything else. We, the Kylr are dying out, there are less babies born every cycle. Kerra and I have had three children together, and so we are the lucky ones. We have both tried with other Kylr and failed to produce anymore. I do not retain Kerra as a companion for only babies, but I am very fond of her, she is stimulating in many ways, and after 231 years of life, I need to be stimulated. We need you two, more than you could ever know. Jillian it would be ideal for you to couple with a Kylr but it is not require to help us. On the other hand Brig We need you to attempt to make a child with Kerra or any of the other Kylr women on board this ship, or all of them if you could" At this Jar stopped and let it sink in.

"Leave us for alone for a little while, please, I want to talk with Jillian alone" Brig said. Jar and Kerra left, but not before Kerra whispered in Jillian's ear and kissed her.

"What was that about?" Brig asked.

"Brig, we have so much to talk about; did you promise Kerra, that you would do anything to save me?" Jillian Inquired.

"You know I did, she already told you. But she didn't have to, you know how I feel, your my life" Brig said flatly.

The hours passed before Jillian and Brig came out of their chamber to find Jar. They ran into the ships officers who were like rowdy sailors, and they made some smart remarks and some of them started to grope Jillian. Instantly Brig lost his calm and the crew nearly lost their lives. If it were not for Jillian soothing Brig's anger the ship would have been torn apart. Jillian was terrified, Brig was so strong and fast and he was glowing with energy. It danced up and down his skin. Brig was always a first rate fighter, never taking any shit form anyone, but he was the first person to just walk away, especially with Jillian present. Not this time.

The infirmary beds were full of crew by the time Kerra showed up. Her assistant, another blue Kylr woman, as goddess-like as Kerra herself was providing medical care to the injured. Kerra looked at the other Dr and something passed between them wordlessly.

The Captain walked in and looked at his men. He turned on a heel and slapped Kerra across her face hard. Before Jillian could blink Brig had the Captain by his throat his body dangling off the ground at the end of Brig's arm. The Captain could not get free despite his much greater size. Brig's eyes were the only thing to give away how furious Brig really was, they were blazing like miniature novas. The captain had blood trickling between Brig's fingers from his collapsed throat and from the broken blood vessels from within it. Kerra who was leaned against the wall where the blow had forced her just looked on without comment.

The crew tried in vain to attack Brig, they were not even

acknowledged as if they were not there at all. Oh they hit and punched Brig as hard as they could, which is much harder that a human do to their superior organs and physiology. Even though, Brig refused them notice. It was the arrival and action of Jar that changed the room. He in a few deft movements had rendered the crew senseless. He then focused on Brig.

"Do you intend to kill him Brigand Sawyer?" Jar asked in a conversational tone, not at all commanding or reproaching.

"I have not decided, he is in no real danger of dying at the moment, this is about education, not elimination." Brig said just as lightly as Jar Had.

"Brig, don't kill him for being a jerk" Jillian said

"No do it because you can" Kerra said "Just kidding, I applaud your chivalry, but I can take this idiot without your assistance. Do let him go."

 The captain hit the floor like a pile of old rags. He was gasping for air and coughing like a old man with COPD, but, he was fine structurally. He regained his feet and turned on Jar with fury in his face.

"How dare he touch me I demand you pun...."

 Kerra hit him so hard in the mouth and then a swiftly knee in the ribs sent the captain on his face moaning.

"Never ever think to lay a hand on me. You are but a lowly captain, I am a member of the supreme council, the head of all medicine and your superior in everyway. I could have your commission revoked and your ass thrown into prison for your trespass, but I wont because of him" Kerra growled, as she pointed at Brig. Jar only smiled slightly.

 The captain was tossed unceremoniously into a bed since he was all beat up. He was very cranky. Once Jar, Brig and the girls left he got his superior tone back.

"I should have stood up and thrashed her" He said.

The female doctor bandaging his neck did not miss a
beat "You got your ass kicked, and would have got it
kicked again if you got up. So shut up and hold still or
I am going to kick you ass." She said. He just sat there
like a spoiled child in a time out.

 The four walked to the observatory to look out at the earth.
No words were spoken for a long time. This was plainly killing
Kerra who was a talk-aholic. Still, Silence was probably best. Jar
did not look at Brig; he was looking at Jillian intensely. She was
aware and finally asked what his thoughts were.

"I am thinking of you Lovely Jillian" Jar said. "You seem to have
a hold over Brig that could be used against him, I don't think that
is wise".

"Don't pursue that Jar; it will lead to heart ache. She is off limits.
If it comes down to it Jillian and I would sacrifice ourselves for
the greater good. I can not be blackmailed or pressed to do what
I know is wrong not even for Jillian" Brig said in an unmistakably
dangerous tone without looking away for the planet below.

    The mood was odd, but not strained. Jillian and Kerra broke it
by comforting the others mate. Jillian went up to Jar and hugged
him. She looked him in the eyes and said "I want us to be very
close friends Jar, and know that I would never betray Brig or you
for any reason. You saved his life so I will pay back that debt by
making sure your honor and standards are not tested over me".
He was startled. "Oh by the way I will never let anyone but Brig
ever be my lover, I truly feel for your people but I am not one of
them and as such I am bound to him and only him. My choice."

"Don't be mad my hero. You are a wonderful bundle of joy when
your mad. I am loving you already for defending me" Kerra told
him with her lips touching his ear. "I really want to bed you and
Jillian and work on a baby, for both of us". It was Brig's turn to be
startled. He had just about popped a man's head like a zit and

this girl wants to talk about sex. He just looked at her as she kissed his cheek.

What happened later that evening was a moment in Kylr history which would prove to be very memorable. The very moment is stuck in time. The crew were patched up and released back to their duties. The captain was leaving the sick bay when he walked by the gallery and noticed something that made his heart stop, The dirty human trash who had dared to place filthy hands on him had a G-jen on his left forearm.

CHAPTER 3: STRANGE ALLIES

The planet Kyl was OH MY GOD beautiful. Jillian had never seen such splendor. She was not here for a sight seeing trip. She, as well as the crew were tossed into hyperspace and launched here by the irate captain who was beside himself. He had gone so far as to lock the ships controls so it could not be over ridden, at least not in the time it took to go from Earth to Kyl. Jar had tried to speak to this man and reason with him. Only fear of Jar kept the discourse civil. In the Captain's mind Jar had betrayed the Kylr people and he must be tried by the supreme council.

When the ship finally landed, no less than ten Guardians came to escort them to the meeting hall. Jillian noticed how nervous they all seemed. She would find out later why. Kerra was verbally lashing the captain for his conduct. She had him arrested for failure to follow a direct order from his superior, namely her. Kerra and Jar were treated well enough, almost like a king and queen.

This was not the case with Jillian and Brig. One of the foolish guards grabbed Jillian's arm and toss-shoved her out into a wall. Brig took him apart in a blink and two of the others Guardians as well. If Jar had not intervened Brig would have put all ten on the shelf, He was furious beyond reason.

"Calm yourself Brig" Jar said as Kerra looked after Jillian.

"She is okay, only bruised" Kerra said angrily, as she looked at the Guard who had done it.

"How dare you touch Jillian, is this your Idea of being a man, is this the great Kylr Guardians you spoke of, I am not impressed" Brig growled through locked teeth.

"What is the meaning of this" Jar said in a calm stern voice?

"The prisoners were resisting" a Guardian explained.

Jar looked at him hard. "Where do you see a prisoner, where indeed. And whom told you there was to be any"?

"They are the prisoners" The guardian stated as Brig lunged at him. Only Jar's strong arm kept the guardian from a beat down.

"Show him" Jar commanded to Brig.

Brig pulled up his left sleeve and all ten Guardians went white with shock, then red with anger. A few took a step forward, but hesitated looking at Jar. He simple stepped out of their way with a twisted grin, which had the effect of unhinging the guardians completely. Brig was more than ready to fight, and hand to hand he was very good, never lost even once. Not even to multiple attackers, he always made them pay dearly for the chance to hurt him. This was such an occasion.

"STOP" Jillian yelled!!! She jumped up and held Brig close to her running her delicate fingers across his face and kissed him on the ear and whispered something.

Brig relaxed, but put his hand up and slowly made a fist, the bone crackled and grated once the fist was closed he squeezed again and the laugh gravel noise it made way as plan as day to all who witnessed it. It was DONT OR ELSE. Petty symbolism maybe but very effective because not a single one of the guard came anywhere near Brig or Jillian as the followed Jar to the Grand structure ahead of them.

The building itself was like the Sydney opera house, only bigger. The reason for its extreme size was simple. It had to hold the many representatives from the different planets. The building was a magical work of art. The engineering that went into it was more art than structure. Everywhere Jillian looked was more beauty and splendor. Brig noticed none of this. He watched the guardians and the regular guards, the exits, every door, every deal. His hunter sense was in full bloom. Kerra noticed that Brig was very close to an explosion and nudged Jar, then looked at Brig. Jar moved closer to Brig, and he looked around in the same fashion as Brig, and he began to see why he was concerned.

They were being hemmed in on all sides. If It were just Brig and himself, he would not worry; but with Jillian and Kerra to look to, he must be careful to control the situation in such a way as to exclude any option to harm the girls.

The supreme council was not happy to be ordered to report to chambers for a special hearing. The subject was treason. This was very distressing. The Kylr were not the betraying kind, a more patriotic loyal race were not to be found in the known universe. Therefore; treason, was the biggest surprise they had ever had in all of their time as counsel members. Moreover, Jar was the one who is accused of treason. This simply can't be so; he is the greatest warrior and most respected Kylr. It is also very important to mention he is beyond their authority...and power. The second item on the table is the well decorated captain of the Kylr flag ship is accused of mutiny and kidnapping, a charge that could bring upon his death if proved. Most, most distressing, all of this thought the chief counselor. No good shall come of any of this. Oh how right he was.

When Jar and Kerra had taken their customary seats in the hall as were afford to their status they were dead center. This was the first time Kerra ever remembered being treated with hostility and anger by her own people, Kerra was one of the most loved and desired friends on Kylr, so she was taken back by the open hostility. Jillian was aware of the tension but acted as if she were not. All those long years of being a model trained her to deal with stress and hostility properly without ever showing her hand. Brig was not so lucky, but only his hansom eyes showed his feelings and Jillian seriously doubted if anyone could read Brig. She could because of a life long love affair with him, their hearts beat as one.

"Well, out with it Guardians. You look as if you wish to attack me" Kerra said. "Why this can be is beyond even my intellect"?

Nobody spoke.

"Very well, hold your piece for now. You will be afforded a time to speak your thoughts" Kerra boldly announced.

The other eleven counsel member filed in and took their seats, all their faces were confused or grim. This was not to their liking. The chairman tapped a tiny bell and the richest sound resonated through the hall. It was exquisite. It made Jillian smile, and Brig relax ever so slightly. He cleared his tiny throat, because he was ancient. His actual age would be impossible to determine without a hint or key or some sort. This in and of itself was unusual from what Kerra said the Kylr were virile until death, yet this fellow was a prune dried in too many days in the sun.

"We will now convene the counsel, the first matter may now be discussed." the chairman said softly, though his little voice was as clear as mountain air to all. "What is the first matter then?"

There was a huge uproar in the side of the great hall as the irate captain burst in the hall screaming. The regular guard were having bad time trying to subdue him. He refused to be coddled or quieted. He struggled and tossed off the guards like fleas off a dogs back. The guardians watched with more than a small interest in the wild spectacle. Jar cleared his throat and a burly Guardian seized the captain by the collar and hoisted him up. He sat the man on the seat directly in front of the chairman. The tiny old fellow with knowing eyes regarded him for a moment, then turned to Kerra.

"Co-chair, would you like to begin with the captains conduct"? The tiny fellow's silky voice asked.

"Yes, I believe it would be proper to begin with that, before we move on to other matters" Kerra calmly stated. "Let the captain make his own statements first".

The captain was taken back by this development, but not enough to be disarmed by it. "I have broken the chain of command, I freely admit to this. I had every right by our laws to do so. Jar and Kerra have committed treason against the Kylr and I need only point in this very room to the result of their foolish actions to defend myself". He turned and pointed at Brig and Jillian.

"They are of the fledgling race on a backwater planet know as Earth. The male has a G-jen on his left arm to prove Jar's treason. The female is with Kerra's child, this proves her treason" the captain stated in a calm law-like fashion.

"That is not possible, we are both Girls" Jillian said.

"Please hold you statements until called upon young one" the tiny fellow added.

"I ask your pardon" Jillian said with a flourish.

The tiny chairman smiled sweetly at Jillian and said "Please go on captain or are you finished"?

"That is enough to begin with but I would like to be allowed to rebut if need be" the captain said.

"Very good, we shall hear from the commander of the Kylr Guardians now, Jar" the tiny fellow said.

"Counsel" Jar stood up and walked to the middle of the room with the counsel on one side and the audience on the other.

"The captain gave an account, yes he did. It left out a great deal of things that are beyond his authority and mental level. He makes very prudent observations, good for a starship captain, but not very good for a scientist or a counsel member which he is not. He has questions Kerra's decisions and actions without knowing what they actually are. I am not going to address that, I will leave it to Kerra herself to explain. The captain has accused me of treason." Jar let the word hang in the room as he turned and viewed all within it, before he began again. "Treason, but what is my treason. Is it visiting earth? Is it saving that man's life? Or it is the fact I placed a G-jen on his arm and made him my student and brother Guardian"?

The room exploded in chaos suddenly and it went on for time with yelling and arguing until Jar had heard enough and let enough venting go, even some of the guardians were bitching.

"Enough"!!!! Jar let his enormous power out briefly and everyone in the room nearly fainted from the pressure in the room except Brig and the tiny speaker chairman who seemed unaffected. Which did not go un-noticed by the Guardians in the assembly hall. "You will be silent" Jar commanded."

"Very nice Jar" said a different looking Kylr. He was a almost female looking guy, he had tight white hair, which is not normal, Kylr males are bald. One more thing he had diamond shaped pupils like a snake, and his eyes were green.

"Do you have something you wish to say Korin" asked Jar.

"Why yes, chief, I do" Said Korin "I stand with you in defense of the Earth man and new Guardian" He pointed at Brig "Earth as you know is in serious danger of attack by any of the carnivore races. However with a Guardian, they will stay their hand for fear of retribution from the mighty Guard. So, I stand for this action that provide Earth with a protector of its own, leaving us to our own work elsewhere". He turned his back to Brig and faced the crowd, with a twisted little smile on his girl like mouth.

"Very well Korin, unexpected, but welcome at any rate" Jar turned back to the counsel, "Shall I continue chairman"? The chairman nodded to go on. "I am no trader, and as Korin stated plainly enough Earth must be protected at all costs, thus I gave the bravest of the brave and the true of heart a G-jen, so that he may lend his strength of character to the protection of his world and the rest of us as well."

The room was about to once more erupt into chaos, but Korin stopped it short. He lifted his left hand and smiled and a pure green light filled the room. More important was Korin's green eyes were ablaze with power. Brig looked at Jar and he seemed worried as did Kerra when Brig looked at her. Who was Korin that they would be worried at his power?

"Be calm brothers and sisters, this is a time of the mind and talk, not strength and combat" He said softly with liquid threat "But if you insist on the later so be it, I have swore to the Earthers as a ally, you would not want me to go back on my word would you" finished Korin.

The Kylr assembled were visibly shaken by Korin's actions.

"I think Kerra should tell us what she knows" Jar said firmly "Before the question of Treason can be fully answered".

"Very good, Kerra would you please address the assembly with your testimony" said the chairman.

Kerra stood up and walked around and sat on the edge of the dais in front of the rest of the counsel. She crossed her legs in a sexy sultry way and she collected her stylus and began to address the crowd.

"It is no secret among the Kylr that fewer and fewer births are coming. It is a fact that if we don't change this, we will die as a race very soon. It is also a fact that we have become immune to most illnesses, so we no longer fear death. With that said, Earth is the answer to our problems, they are genetically compatible with us in every way. If we mix with them, we will save ourselves and enrich their world at the same time" Kerra explained.

"SEE, TREASON" Screamed the captain.

The room would likely have erupted into chaos and arguing, but Korin was still radiating a green aura and they kept their thought to a conversational tone and none made any kind of move to attack Kerra or the Earth people. Jar though glad at Korin's support was still nervous at it, for a reason undisclosed.

"Treason, bah! Is it treason to save our people, and continue the Kylr, I think not. If you profess to know more about medicine than I; then you may have my seat on the counsel" Kerra said with anger.

The crowd as one gave a sharp gasp at Kerra's assertion.

The chairman merely smiled and waved gently that Kerra was to still have the floor. She smiled and slightly bowed to him.

"I have performed experiments with Jillian's DNA, more to the point, her eggs. I fertilized it with Brigand's seed and it grew...inside of me. (Gasps) I took it upon myself to see to the continuation of our race. By implanting the fertilized egg in myself, the baby will be mingled with my blood, thus it will get the genetic gifts of the Kylr but the vitality of the father and other mother from Earth." Kerra explained. "Jar wanted to do the same in reverse to Jillian for the good of our race but I would not allow it, without her permission."

"So, you stole part of me to help you, nice. I didn't know I was a supermarket, for you to go to and take what you need. Wise of you however, Kerra not to put a baby in me that is not Brig's, because it is his children alone I will have or nobodies. However," Jillian said calming herself "since you saved my life I don't blame you for trying to do the same for yourselves, so no harm done".

"What of the Earth man, will he help to fertilize us again. He is now a Guardian and will live a great long time, and many new babies could spring from him, if he will agree" The chairman said in his silky voice?

"Well" Brig started as he looked at Jillian "Kerra and Jar did broach the subject, but our way is more private than the Kylr, we are shy by your standards. I am however, bound to a promise made to Kerra to help her in anyway she requires as long as it does not hurt Jillian".

The crowd and the counsel broke up to discuss the events such as they were. The Guardians looked over Brig and Jillian but stayed several arm lengths away from them, because Korin was standing between them smiling. Korin seemed to be very interested in Brig and Jillian. Friendly, would be a understatement, but not overbearing just very chummy.

Jillian actually liked Korin and found the affectionate way he was to be endearing. Brig was strangely drawn to Korin and that made him very uncomfortable, He only felt drawn to Jillian, and now Korin. Brig thought it was the G-jen on his wrist that caused this. He was however wrong about that which he would learn.

Finally, the counsel came out and the chairman; who was named Jamis the wise one; called the counsel to order and remained standing. He looked down from the dais and took in Jillian and then Brig slowly, before he spoke.

"We have a dilemma children. You see it is forbidden to place a G-jen on a non Kylr, no matter how just the cause. You could turn on us and you are more powerful than you know son. You my dear are equally dangerous to us because you represent life, our life continued. Thus, hope. You both know of us and where we are, so here in lies the issue. What to do with you" Jamis said softly but with concern. "What would you have us do about you?"

Jillian was about to plead, when Brig held up a hand and stopped her from continuing.

"We did not ask for this, any of this and I will not allow you to harm my Jillian. And you are completely incorrect about what I know sir. I for instance know not even Jar could take my life, nor for that matter could Korin or any number of Guardians. If they tried..." The entire build and miles around began to vibrate with power, Brig's power. It was red and very like Korin's. Just as it began it stopped. "I can defend on a level few could match, and none could over come. Only death would stop me. So, it is you and not I who must decide... war or peace. Trust or not. It is your choice as the host. But know this even as a tiny boy I have had an unbreakable spirit, and would fight for what is right and Just, no matter the size of the task or opponent, I am undaunted" Brig told them in earnest.

"What do you say young lady" Jamis asked kindly?

"I am with Brig, as in all things, in life or death we are of one mind, one heart" Jillian said flatly. She expected a fight and knew she was a liability to Brig who was as skilled a combatant as they come. She could do nothing but lend her support for what he must do alone.

"I told you it would be thus Jamis, they are strong" Said Kerra.

"The it is my judgment" Jamis began.

The entire went off like a green neutron bomb. From the dust a great green raptor-like bird rose screeched and vanished.

CHAPTER 4: A NEW LIFE SURPRIZE.

In the hills of the gorgeous mountain ranges on Kylr, three lonely figures sit around a fire feeling each other out. The tide that brought them here is all but a memory. However, the result is not. Brig looks at his companions and knows there will be hell to pay in the end from this. They had ran for it, well, actually Korin took them to safety against Brig's will. In the end this was what was best for Jillian really. Brig's bruised honor was a small thing to pay for Jillian's life; and he would pay it as many times as it took.

Korin was in a good humor as usual, nothing seemed to phase him at all. He sat talking to Jillian in a very jovial way. She seemed to be very taken with Korin, Brig for the first time in his life was at the very least somewhat jealous, which was a new thing for him.

Brig looked at the G-jen on his arm and not for the first time wondered if all of these new things were directly related to it. He had never known blind anger or jealousy or unwanted aggression.

Yes, the G-jen must be it. Brig was a gentle soul, he would never hurt anything without cause, except where Jillian was involved, in that way he was all teeth and claws. He had never smothered her. She was free to come and go as she pleased; and he would wait for her if that was her wish. Lucky for him she wanted him as strongly as he wanted and needed her. Yes, needed. Brig was not the type of person to fight or even stand up for himself; he became that as a small boy when he met Jillian. It made something inside of him break like a Dam holding back a ocean.

When the local bully made Jillian cry, it made the shy tiny boy's heart break, and the tiger from within came out, and with it an attitude that felt no pain, no remorse and no mercy. Brig gave no quarter and ask none. He had not spoken, he went silently to work destroying his enemy. Words were not needed only results. Thus Brigand Sawyer became know to live up to his given name...Brigand, mean bandit or hard cased. He remained shy to this day, but the tiger only sleeps waiting to be call on.

Korin was watching Brig with a strange wanton expression that Jillian thought seemed a crush. Which confused her and amused her at the same time. Brig was not phobic of a single thing but he was not gay and this would be new for him, and he being a gentle person would not want to injure Korin's feelings by rudeness. She would have to wait to see how it all played out. More still, it seemed to her that Korin was flirting with her as well, thus there was confusion about the signals.

"Your G-jen is unique as is mine" Korin said suddenly. "It is very rare and made by the old master who created the very Guardians, which we now are. He is a great man and I admire him greatly. His kindness and wisdom are to be aspired to."

"Jar" Brig asked?

"Jar" (hysterical laughter) "Oh, God no! Jar, please, that pompous man. Sorry, Jar is a great man, really. He is just not my ideal for wisdom or kindness. I love him I suppose,(Korin made an odd face here) but as a brother and mentor, but that is the limit of it. No, the old one who created the G-jen was more than a man; he was a genius and a father to all of us".

They sat and listened to Korin as he explained the history of the Kylr people. Once along time ago other of the great races, meat eaters, came to Kyl and began to kill and eat their people. They tried in vain to fight, but were no match for the invaders, who slaughter thousands and enslaved and raped the female of the race. That is until one day a small, elderly man hatched a daring plan. He would challenge The Grot commander to a duel if he lost; then his life would be forfeit and the Kyl would surrender. Well, you can imagine how that went over. It didn't. The people had no faith in a tiny old man, how could he of all of them best a 600lbs Grot warrior, little alone the commander. You see the Grot achieve rank by force of arms, therefore the more dangerous and skilled the fighter the higher the rank. A commander was the best of the best, a natural born killer.

Needless to say Korin had both of his companions glued to their seats. He went on. The Tiny old fellow decided that if the Kylr were to be saved, he alone must risk it all. If the people did not support him then, they could rebel not having agreed to the bargain. As expected the Grot were bound by a warrior tradition to except any challenge no matter how obviously absurd.

The Grot gathered in a great circle of giants, for compared to the Kylr, they are just that. An average Grot is 8 foot and 500lbs, the commander was 600lbs and well over 9 feet. The tiny 5ft Kylr man who perhaps might have tipped the scale at 150lbs was almost missed among the rabble when he entered the ring. What happened next is a thing of legend.

The Grot spoke loudly "You know the law, nobody interferes or enters the ring, to the victor goes the spoils, no retribution if I loose" He growled! "And when I win I eat alone" he laughed.

"You shall loose" screamed the little man who burst into flames and flew into the face of the Grot.

The Grot, incase you are not familiar with their species, are very hardy and damned hard to injure little alone kill. Nonetheless this onslaught was so fast and powerful it toppled the Grot to the ground. He rolled and regained his feet in a well rehearsed move. He could only stare in admiration at his tiny foe. He had never been bull tackled to the ground, and yet a waif of a man did just that. He stood to his full height and looked down at the tiny Kylr. He clapped.

"Well done, it is a pity I have to kill you. I am impressed by your attack. Do you think I could see it again, or is that a one time shot" the Grot leader said with true respect in his voice.

"Yes, I can and will just for you. I ask you this once more yield and leave this planet forever, before I am forced to kill you" whispered the Kylr man.

"Sadly, I cannot. You see we are hungry and you taste good to us, we don't like killing for food, we are fighters and this brings us no glory. Only life" the Grot commander said gently.

"Very well, you shall not have to decide then, The Kylr are off the menu". At that moment the Kylr man shot up and hard left, caught the Grot up under the chin by his ear and toppled him again.

The Grot as a race are use to fighting all the time, but this was different, none of them could do once what the wee man did twice. Moreover, how was he flying and where did you power come from? They were now very interested in the battle, where moments before they were just waiting for the kill. Some were even shouting encouragement to the Kylr man. Betting broke out on when the man would make a mistake and buy the farm. The commander got up and was still smiling, if anything Brighter than before. He loved a challenge. What began as a farce was now a full on contest; and he was loving it. The Kylr made another pass and then several more.

The leader was bleeding a little but not much, and he was having no signs of weakness or Fatigue. After what seemed like forever to the blood thirsty Grot crowded around the Commander after he landed a single hard blow that sent the tiny foe spiraling out of the air into the ground. The Grot roared and lunged forward to be stopped short by the commanders roar of anger.

"He fought well, you will not trample him or touch him. If he still lives I shall grant him a warrior death quick and clean". Said the very large winner of the contest. He walked over and stood looking down at the tiny Kylr who fought so well and sighed with sadness.

"You did very well but you never really had a chance to win, I bid you a fond farewell little brother, you should have been born a Grot your spirit cries for battle".

To have utter surprise the tiny man was laughing. He got to his hands and knees still gasping for breath; because he was have a riot of laughter. He finally got to his feet and the Grot all gasped.

Not a single mark of injury was upon him. In fact, he was fresh as a daisy. He too was smiling a little smile. The Grot commander approached him, but not to attack. He just knelt down and looked him over. He went as far as asking the man to turn in a circle so he could see all of him. Truly there was no injury of any kind. The commander seemed baffled. He looked around and walked up to a huge boulder and punched it. It exploded into a million pieces under the force of his blow.

"I am very powerful, rocks crush under my hand; yet a mighty killing blow from my fist leaves no mark on you. How can this be my friend?" the commander asked in confusion. "I should be able to crush you easily."

"NO, you were never even in this fight" The Kylr man pointed his hand at a small hill of giant boulders and made a fist and all the rocks were crushed to sand suddenly under his power.

"I had hoped to show you that fighting is not your only option, you have another course you can take. There is no hope of defeating me, I am all powerful, I can kill all of you at once if I so choose that way" once again pointed to where the rocks had once been. "I do not want that, leave now and come only in peace or you will be killed by the Guardians of Kyl" he said sternly for the first time as to bake no crumb of defiance.

"Your display of power is as you say nothing we can combat, so I beg you kill me, because I can not live and loose a challenge. It is our law, I am a commander and therefore I am the one who is to enforce that very law" The Grot said sadly but with a deep sense of pride, "I feel no shame at the outcome, you are my better and I am yours to dispose of".

"Am I to understand you correctly by saying your life belongs to me" the Kylr asked?

"That is so" the commander said, still kneeling.

"Then such as it is, I may take your life one day, but this is not that day. I order you to withdraw all the Grot and guard this planet until we can defend it on our own" The tiny man said.

"Alas I can't comply. I gave an oath when I took this mission, I can not go back on my word even for death" The Grot said.

"What specifically was your mission", ask the Kylr man?

"To find a new food source, meat in specific. Our own planet is small compared to this one and the wild game have been played out, so are the fish, so it is a new source of meat or starvation" the commander stated.

"OH MY GOD, is that why you slaughter my people" The Kylr man fumed and shook with anger and anguish "IDIOTS, we would have gladly given you gaming and fishing privileges if you only asked. Kyl is a huge world and is vigorous with life. So, if your world could support itself, would your specific mission be fulfilled"?

"Yes, and we could return home with honor" the Grot said.

"DONE!" exclaimed the tiny man.

The Kylr man had all of the Grot troops gather around him. They did not know why but given the power in this tiny being they did not argue. The world around turned blue because of the tiny blue sun that was once a Kylr man in the middle of them. They could feel the immense power pulsating through them and it was both exhilarating and terrifying at the same instant. The Blue sun looked to the heavens and a blue pulse shot from him into the sky. All of the Grot war host were caught and froze in place immobile; that is not even the strange part. They could feel memories coming back of hunting and fishing, all of them.

Suddenly, they could move and the little man was laying on the ground at their feet so very still. For the first time in history, they felt admiration and pity.

True to their word the entire Grot host; including the few killed by the Kylr were taken aboard the Grot ships, but only after the little blue man was buried like a king, as was his right by combat. The commander cried at his lost foe's funeral. Never had he know such valor, it shamed him to be compared to this unlikely hero.

When the Grot ships landed on the Home world of the Grot, the commander was ordered to the palace for an audience with the king himself. It was to the commander's mind a death order, because his mission failed. To his utter astonishment, he was greeted as a hero and the king hugged him like a son.

"You have saved us" The king crooned, "Word of your deeds are carved on the great rock walls of the Ipsun cliffs, would you like to see it yourself"?

"Yes, Sire I would" The commander said humbly.

The trip out to the cliffs on the royal skimmer only a short time. The shock at what was there on the cliffs would last a life time and longer. There before them was a glass smooth wall of rock that was once rough and deadly to climb. On the surface of the rock were glowing blue words burnt into the rock face.

They were an account of the commander's exploits and triumphs. They were blarney, a total fabrication, but they were so beautiful to read and look upon; the guilt that the commander felt washed away.

"See for yourself, it promises game will return to the land, and fish to the seas and rivers and so it has. There are new game here that have never been know on Grot Prime, this is your doing. More, the Ministry of science tells me the planet has grown to ten times the size it has been. How was this done" asked the King?

"If I told you truly Sire you would not believe me, so I speak thus, I met a powerful being on the planet where I was sent and he bargained with me. In leu of eating his people he would restock our own world with game, fish and other things. The enlargement of our beloved planet was a unexpected boon" The Commander said plainly. "Here me now my king, we are to never set foot on his planet again, so mighty is he that from millions of parsecs away his bent our planet to his will and brought back life, and new life as well. We are no match for this, I gave my word to never return unless in peace with friendship in my heart".

"You have made us a bargain that is just and correct. I wonder though if we could bend this being to our will, we could rule the universe" the King pondered. He could see the mighty Commander was uneasy and decided that it was likely a fatal effort, so he dropped it as it should be.

"I wish to honor you Commander. I have no son or daughter and my years grow long, I am still strong and able to make war but; when my time comes I would have a good head on the throne...Yours" The king said as he looked hard into the commanders eyes to gauge his thoughts.

"I am unworthy, but I can not refuse your request as you know best" The Commander whispered.

"Good, done. You are now Prince Grot-Elor or Elor if that suits you, and you are my son now, and answer to me alone, you are above all but my laws. Do you understand this? I want you to deal with all off world issues and bring our troops to heel son." The king said joyfully. He seemed to think that Elor might refuse him and was visually shaken by the thought.

The Kylr unearthed the grave of the elder and it was empty.

They were horrified at the thought of the Grot taking the elders body back with them. However, they watched as the Grot Commander laid the Body to rest and spoke soft words of a fallen warrior and hero. It was quite moving. Who would have thought a blood thirsty monster like the Grot could be so eloquent and show grace at a tender time. The problem now was, where is the body of the elder who saved them all; and what now?

"Why do you stand around when there is work to be done to fix the damage done by the Grot invasion?" Said a soft booming voice?

The People turned and had a collective intake of breath. For there sitting on top of a rock, glowing like the sun itself was the recently killed little blue elder. He smiled in a fatherly way at them, and their lack of understanding. They did not approach him as they believed him dead and that made them wary of him.

"Silly children, did you think I played with the lives of our people so recklessly. I knew from the get-go, I would prevail and we would be free of our invaders", Said the elder.

"But we saw you die" said a voice in the crowd?

"A harmless trick, simple with my G-jen. It seemed that I was lost to the veil, but, alas no. I was pretending to get them to leave us. I did not want to slaughter them for the crime of stupidity, so I set them on a better path, one that does not have us on the menu" chuckled the elder.

Thus the golden age of Kyl began under the elder's easy guidance, we as a people made the giant leap forward as a race. He one day showed us all his G-jen. It was a strange glowing gauntlet on his right arm. It was both Beautiful, and omni-powerful. We had no fear though because he was a gentle father figure who used kindness to steer us and joy with our every achievement. In time he made a second G-jen and presented it to Jar and young Kylr male with high moral fiber and a good level head on his shoulders. The elder is the only one knows to be able to remove his G-jen and not die. He lives to this day to keep us upon the course of justice and intelligence.

The night lights from the distance danced in Brig's eyes as he prepared to face his future.

CHAPTER 5: TO DECIDE

In the great hall Jar was addressing the crowd of angry Kylr who had gathered to demand Brig and Jillian be hunted down and dealt with. Jar knew that Brig had not run for it. This was Korin's doing. That fool would ruin Kerra's and his plans to save their race. Still he envied Korin's pluck, never had there been another such as Korin, of all the guardians that could have thrown in with Brig, Korin was one of the few that the others would not challenge. Well, not without a lot of back up and good cause, Korin was humorous and friendly openly. However, Korin was a most Intractable advisory, deadly and merciless when engaged. Jar was troubled though, why had Korin swept away the humans?

"Find them and punish them, or enslave them. I would personally like a shot at some private time with the girl, very fetching" said a brute of a guardian.

"No thanks, filthy Earthers should be put to death, not bred with. Has Kerra lost her mind" said a thin wiry Kylr named Miko." Rok, do you think that Brig fellow would let you taste his woman's pleasures? And then there is Korin...NO, I will not face that nutcase, it would be certain death or a year of painful healing".

The large brute name Rok said "Miko my little friend you are way too concerned by Korin".

"I am not the one with a green firebrand scar on my back marking me as the fool who underestimated Korin" Miko pointed out.

"True" Rok admitted suddenly thinking deeply on the subject.

Jar seeing that this was the proper moment to interject stepped forward and raised his hand. All of the Guardians came to focus on him in that instant.

"I would have you wait and hold your opinions until you have heard Jamis speak his decision and that of the grand counsel to you from his own lips, so that it is not refutable" Jar said in a hard tone. He turned and looked at Jamis with a slight bow.

The old speaker stood with no effort and smiled in his usual kindly way. He did something that the guardian had never seen before; he levitated over the dais and to the floor among them. What power is this that lifted the speaker; some thought to themselves.

"I wish for you to look into my face from near it, and understand that I must be obeyed in this decision of ours. You will indeed find the human children and bring them back. Beware, the G-jen of Korin is among the most powerful ever created and Korin knows its use well. Brigand Sawyer; knows not the full extent of his G-jen but his will and metal must NOT be tested, Jar has shown me the soul of this fighter and if engaged he will fight to the death and never will you beat a man such as him with power alone, therefore engage them not. Your mission is to approach and convince them to come of their own will" said Jamis.

"It will be difficult for Korin will not let you near them" Kerra said with a chuckle "I feel Korin wants them all to Korin and no other. Sad, I want to enjoy them as well, but no matter. Listen carefully. Korin has taken to the hills where none could hope to over match him, if you go in guns blazing Korin will kill you. Announce yourself or sneak in and take Jillian, but fight not the male, for his fury is a truly monstrous thing, so is dear Korin's". She made a serious face then spun on a heel and left toward her own labs.

"Does she think us children to be told our lot in life, we are guardians and know well our duty" Miko said in a haughty voice.

"Then stop acting like children and mark her advice well, for it will save your life." Jamis said sternly, with no smile this time stealing the thunder from Miko. Jamis was never to be questioned.

"Jamis, it takes a great deal to kill one of us, why do you think that this Earther could do it, Korin I will admit could likely end any of us, though I am not sure how. Korin is a mystery to us granted, but past experience tells me that the more dangerous the mission the more Korin wanted it. Korin has never failed in combat at any level, practice or practical, so, I will be ready if I must face him. But of the other I know nothing sir, and I feel we must if we are to bring them here" Rok asked.

The elder speak pondered his answer for a short time, not because his mind was slow, quite the opposite was true. No, he didn't know how to explain without telling too much. He finally made up his mind looking Rok straight in the eye.

"His G-jen is special, it carries with it many special abilities that can be troublesome to you if they are used. If Brig looses his temper the G-jen will empower him with a terrible force that none could stand against, so cause no anger children, be at peace with him and ask him to come back with you" Jamis said.

"If he resists do we have leave to kill him or Korin" Miko asked?

"I may never see you again Miko, if you try that against those two" Jamis said plainly. The elder Speaker shimmered and disappeared.

"Was then that a yes or a no" Miko asked confused?

"NO" Jar growled at him. "Rok, you go fetch them alone, Miko will just get you killed if he goes along. Why he wants to fight Brig is beyond me"?

"Maybe a lot of things are beyond you these days Jar, maybe your head is going soft and maybe your day of leading is over" Miko said.

He would have said more but Jar's fist hit him between the eyes, sending him spiraling into the wall with a crack. He got up with blood dripping from his left eye. Miko seethed with hatred but, was not fool enough to try the Mighty Jar, he was angry not stupid.

The forests of Kyl were gorgeous. The wildlife were a wide variety of spectacular. Jillian walked next to Korin and asked a million questions. Brig saw the trees, animals and splendor as a distraction from the hell that was coming. He therefore, could not enjoy it or let his guard down. A sudden movement in the brush caught and held Brig's attention.

A burst of color shot from the brush and landed on Brig's shoulder. Brig would have reacted but Korin grabbed his arm and stayed his hand.

"It is a Wira Monkey, they are rare and never touch anyone unless they are willing to bond with them, which is even more rare. You are twice blessed my friend" Korin chimed.

"Great" Brig said in a groan. He just looked at the tiny creature and sighed in resignation and began to walk on behind Jill.

"Are they dangerous, Korin" Jillian asked?

"Oh, yes they are, but only if your it's enemy" Korin said and then laughed at Brig's face when he looked at the Wira on his shoulder.

"What could this little monster do, he is small and helpless" Brig asked.

Korin stopped and looked at him hard "You are small Brigand Sawyer, are you helpless, have you no teeth and claws with which to fight. No, Yes? Think of your own self, then apply that knowledge to the Wira on your shoulder" Korin offered with a bland face. He turned and kept on the way he was going, catching Jillian by the wrist pulling her along.

The little monkey had big red eyes with yellow pupils, it was soft as silk and warm to the touch. It looked into Brig's eyes and seemed to see what it was looking for.

"Breeg" the Wira said. "Breeg, Oru, Breeg".

"What, did you say my named lil fella" Brig asked?

"He said Brig my Brig. Oru is likely it's name" Korin said
without a pause in step or looking back.

Jillian pulled her hand from Korin's and waited for Brig to
catch up. Korin was angry about something, Brig was paying no
heed to it, likely, because he was worried about her so the hell
with Korin. Oru was nuzzling Brig's head, and Brig was actually
enjoying it from the look of it. In fact both of them began to
giggle. A snap fast bolt of green fire shot right at the Wira. At the
last moment the monkey swung away avoiding the impact by
diving into the brush.

"WTF, is wrong with you" Brig snapped at Korin "What if you hit
Jillian, and you tried to kill my new friend. He better be okay or
your going to get such a pinch dude!"

The forest erupted in a flurry of action as a huge monster
ripped into Korin with the force of a charging Rhino. Korin spun
swiftly to meet the charge head on. Leaves and dirt flew
everywhere and when it settle Korin was holding the monster by
one tusk of two that jutted out of the corners of the monsters
mouth. It was a huge muscular humanoid.

"ORU" Brig said and the monster's eyes shifted to him. "Oh wow
it is you. Man, did you grow up big."

"Breeg" It growled and flung Korin like a doll away as it ran to
Brig's side and picked him up. The giant purred like a small fluffy
toy at Brig.

"Wow, that is some change Oru made" Jillian said.

"Tell me about it, I think he busted my ribs hugging me so hard"
Brig said with a chuckle.

"Still think Oru helpless" Korin asked?

"No, I guess not. But how did he get so big so fast, I mean zero to 800lbs in like 2 seconds flat, that has to be a record or something" Brig blurted!

"Oru is a Lasomorph, a being that can change its body mass and structure to meet any situation or need. If Oru thought I was really a serious threat to you, I would be forced into a deadly combat" Korin said with a smile.

    The sudden drop in crushing pressure from Oru's mega hug caused Brig to look sharply at Oru. The huge creature was slowly shrinking and morphing back into a tiny monkey creature. The tusks were the first thing to disappear, and then the bulk of the Wira shifted in an almost inward way, as if there was a tiny singularity within the monkey swallowing the extra parts as they shifted. A shocked look on the face of Jillian said that she saw the same thing and was baffled how it all worked?

    The spectacle of the Wira changing was enough to capture and hold Brig and companies attention but at that moment a Guardian drop heavily on to the ground 15 feet from Jillian. She jumped back startled at the size of the brute. He stood up, come off his knee from the impact. Korin snapped a fast right hand up and aimed at the intruder, but stopped short of any action, eyes darting around glowing with green power. Brig went into full combat mode. Violent red flames ripped off his every inch. The Wira changed to a red scaled dragon like creature in an instant and was standing ready beside Brig.

"No, Wait" Korin yelled, diving between Brig and the guardian.

"What is it Korin, why not drop this joker before he is set to Fight?

"Rok, what do you want here, and where is Miko" Korin asked?

    Brig took a full on blast of raw energy in his back. Oru jumped away and turned invisible.

"See, I told ya Rok we could take them" Miko said grabbing Jillian.

"Oh My GOD!" Korin said as he tackled Rok to the ground.

Where Rok had been standing was now polished smooth as glass by the energy coming off Brigand Sawyer. Rok did not even struggle with the tiny Korin he just caught his breath and threw up a defensive barrier to save himself from being cooked alive by the heat wave.

"Muther Fucker" came the low dangerous rumble from inside of Brig's throat. He began to move but suddenly he stopped and saw Jillian in Miko's grip. Miko smiled as if he had the upper hand...he stopped smiling when Brig began to slowly pointed at Miko's face.

"Don't' or your bitch will get it first" Miko said. Then he suddenly began to choke and fell to his knees. Oru appeared behind him with his tail wrapped around Miko's neck, tightening it more every second.

"Nu keel Breeg" Oru rasped between giant razor teeth! Then tossed Miko like a half eaten apple aside, and vanished again. It was very un-nerving, because he could strike and you were helpless. Wira were powerful at a guardian's level, and more when pressed to protect a bondling, like Brig for instance. Miko was lucky the Oru noticed Brig was ok, or his head would have been torn off.

"So you came to off us huh" Korin said just before he engulfed Rok in emerald flames "You will not succeed" Korin finished.

"STOP, PLEASE KORIN" Rok cried!!! "I didn't know Miko followed me, I SWEAR!"

"Wait, Korin. Let him talk, we need to know what these asses are doing here, and if we need to watch for more of them" Jillian whispered from the crux of Brig's neck where her face was buried. Brig nodded his agreement.

"Very Well" Korin said, though his eyes burned with battle lust. "Speak."

The near giant Rok relaxed visibly and composed himself as if the speech would be of great importance to them. Korin's eyes flash dangerously at the obvious delay. Rok stepped on the gas so to speak.

"The Elder Jamis has sent me to fetch you back to him, He further told me not to engage you in battle. I have not done so, as those were my orders. I go further and apologize for Miko, whom was told not to come along by Jar and Jamis alike. He disobeyed. I offer you no threat or trickery" Rok said sternly.

"Well Korin, you know these people and we do not, is his word trust worthy or are you going to destroy him" Brig asked turning to look at Korin fully?

"I have never known Rok to let an un-truth spring from his lips, he is rigid in his sense of right and wrong and duty as well. Miko, on the other hand is a Sonuva...well not to be trusted on any level" Korin said as he released Rok from the green hell.

Jillian looked around and saw Miko's bleeding form flanking them, before she could utter a word a beam of pure destruction was launched at Brig's back. Like chained lightning Rok moved in a blur and took the brunt of the blow on himself. The impact tossed him spiraling uncontrollably into the brush.

"No not Rok" Miko screamed in anguish as one of his few friend went down hard.

The next instant everything seemed to be in slow motion as Korin shifted, stopping in-front of Miko. He said nothing. Miko also did not speak, only took one step back. Both of the guardians tossed the hand containing the G-jen out as the power came to bear on their opponent. The battle was very short. For all the power Miko had at his command, it was only a drop in the ocean compared to Korin's might. Korin seemed supernaturally calm and focused. Korin did the last thing that Miko ever thought and that cost him his worthless life as a back jumper and a coward; so, Miko was slain quickly and efficiently.

Meanwhile Jillian ran to where Rok had been thrown to see if he was still alive. He was laying in an impossible position wedged into trees. His massive body was going to work against him in his current predicament. Jillian tried to get him out but it was beyond her.

"ORU HELP" she screamed!

Oru became visible right beside Jillian. She did not even flinch, the creature instilled in her confidence and calm, so her mind was on the task of trying to save Rok's life. Oru reached forward and lifted Rok out of the spot where he was wedged with surprising care and gentleness. Oru placed the torn up guardian on the ground at Jillian's feet, and backed away. Jillian stepped around Rok and placed a hand on the Wira's head.

"Thank you Oru" Jillian said kindly.

"Jilleee pleeezed" Oru crooned?

"Yes, very" she answered.

The body of Miko was placed on the ground beside Rok by Korin. There was no stride made to try to help Miko, who was thoroughly dead. All efforts were being made by the group to save Rok from death.

"Korin can you help him" Brig asked "He saved my life, so he can't die as a reward."

"This is beyond my knowledge if not my power Brigand Sawyer. We need Jamis" Korin said.

"Then it is settled, we go back" Jillian said with a tone that brooked no argument.

They picked up their gear. Korin grabbed the corpse of Miko. Oru, unbidden gently lifted Rok into his mighty fur covered arms. Brig held onto Jillian. In a flash of green light they were gone.

CHAPTER SIX: RETURN VISIT.

The lab where Kerra was overseeing medical research was busy and laughter could be heard from a distance. Kerra was a big fan of free expression. She believed it was a precursor to creativity, and in research that is a must. Still, she was feeling uneasy every since Jar had informed her that Korin whisked Brig and Jillian away. Oh Kerra trusted Korin with her life and knew more about Korin than anyone. Still, it was a dangerous time for the humans and her people. All the futures of the main players were lining up. It would be salvation or ruination soon. Kerra had high hopes and low expectations, as always she planned for the worst and prayed for the best.

The counsel chamber found Jar and Jamis in a heated discussion. Jar had just informed the honored Elder speaker of Miko's disobedience and interference. Jamis was outlining his feelings on the matter, Jar was not in agreement.

"We should send out a few teams to arrest Miko before all hell loose, you know he can be an arrogant idiot. It was a sad day when he was given a G-jen" Jar said with conviction.

"No, that we should not do Jar. It would only start a war among the children. We want to embrace the Earth and it's children as well as ours. If we interfere it will likely drive a wedge of prejudice between our peoples, and we can not afford that. I will hope that between Rok and Korin there is enough good report that they can negate Miko's stupidity" Jamis calmly explained.

They would have continued their disagreement but the room shook and a storm of green fire filled the room.

(RUMBLE....KA-BOOM)

"Jamis, you are needed desperately" Korin shouted.

It was Jar who reacted first, and in the wrong way. He saw Oru holding the limp body of Rok and assumed that he had been attacked by the creature. So Jar attacked. Oru not wanting to let any harm come to Rok, turned his back to the guardian and just absorb the brunt. Blood sprayed all over the room and Oru did not try to move or fight back. He just stood in place shielding Rok's broke body in his arms.

"Drop him beast or I will slay you where you stand" Jar screamed at Oru. These were the last words he said before the world turned.

A tornado hit Jar, So fast were the blows that he as powerful as he was could not defend himself. Knees, fists, feet, elbows and even head butts rained down on Jar like damnation itself. Jar tried to ascertain who could attack at this level. He believed it was Korin at first, thinking only Korin had the back bone, speed and power for such an onslaught. But he was wrong. Brig grabbed him by the trachea, twisted in a neat move and bull slammed him face first into the polished marble floor. Before Jar could counter or stop the attack, Brig grabbed his left ankle and catapulted him into the far wall. Jar hit so hard the stone powdered under the impact. Jar dazed by the sheer force of the beating thus far thought to have an instant to catch his breath because of the distance he had just been thrown. He was wrong, so utterly and terrible incorrect. The moment Jar hit the wall Brig hit him again in the chest like a rampaging rhino. The wall gave way and both men went threw.

"Brig NO, NO...Don't kill him" Jillian and Kerra yelled in unison!

Jar was beaten within a thread of his life. Never had anyone in the universe bested him, little alone destroy him so utterly. Jar looked up at Brig and was startled to see the transformation. Brig was a crimson cloud of pure rage, on the verge of a psychotic break. He reached down and grabbed Jar by the throat and pulled him up slowly, painfully slowly for effect. When they were nearly nose to nose he spoke.

"If Oru dies so do you" Brig growled low and menacing. He

dropped Jar unceremoniously on his butt and turned to Jillian.

"Never mind me, see to Oru Brig" Jillian said briskly.

Brigand Sawyer, with a slight nod of compliance walked by her and Kerra with no more attention paid to them than a stranger in a busy city would get.

"Hey buddy let me look at what you got here" Brig said to Oru, who was mewing in pain. "Korin please attend to Rok's needs. Oru give Rok to Korin, so he can get well. You have done well I am proud of you".

"Oru-gaza, me-gaza ruu. Splendid my friend" Korin said as he ruffle Oru's neck fur, then took Rok from him.

"Korin-gaza, Rok-gaza leev, heeelp heeeem" Oru wheezed as blood came out his mouth.

Brig's head turn only slightly to regard Jar in the corner with his left eye, but they rise in power and temperature could be felt miles away. Jar and Kerra shuttered. Jamis however seemed to take all of this in stride.

The elder walk over to where Korin was laying Rok on a medical platform. He inspected Rok and looked trouble for a moment. He looked hard at Korin. Korin stared back just as hard. Jamis turned and scanned the room. His eyes came to rest on the bundle that was Miko's dead body. Jamis looked at Korin, this time Korin nodded his head.

"I will require a full account Korin, of your adventures and what became of Miko" Jamis said in an even tone.

"I will be ready at the appointed time master" Korin said with respect. Korin showed respect to nobody, so this was odd for him.

Kerra came over to where Brig was examining Oru, and got on her knees to look at the damage. It was bad, perhaps terminal even with proper medical care. Brig has a strange look on his face as his eyes locked on to Oru's. It seemed to Kerra that Brig and Oru were speaking in their minds to each other. Was that possible?

Brig looked at Jar and narrowed his eyes and spoke very, very softly.

"Come're".

The commander of the Guardian flew across the floor like a fish on the line. Brig placed his G-Jen encase hand on Jar's G-jen and took a breath.

(Scream)!!!

Jamis turned around with a start, eyes as wide as pie plates. He watched Brig do the near impossible. Brig stole the power and vitality out of Jar to regenerate the wounds that he had inflicted on Oru. Jar was out of his mind in pain, but did not seem to Jamis to be dying or even in danger of it. Thus Jamis turned and attended to Rok who was in dire need of his special attentions.

Hours later in the private chambers of the elders of Kylr, Jamis was holding court, well sort of. The aged speaker was questioning the adventurers over refreshments.

"Korin what happened to Miko" Jamis asked?

"We were camping in the wilds and having a good visit, getting to know about each other. Miko decided to ambush us, and take Jillian hostage. Well, he made the error of threatening Brig and the Wira took Jillian away from Miko and beat the taste out of his mouth, but did not kill him, at Jillian's request. Rok stumbled into camp and I disabled him. He explained that he was sent to fetch us by you Jamis and he had not come to fight, so I released him. Miko not wanting to be beaten, his pride wounded, attempted to kill Brig and Jillian by a second ambush. Rok saw it coming and jumped into the way saving Brig and Jillian. That is what happened to Dear Rok. Miko had pressed his luck with me once to often. I faced him and broke the link between him and his G-jen, killing him" The green eyed Guardian produced Miko's G-jen and gave it to Jamis; and then Korin reached for a donut hole.

"Oru helped Jillian rescue Rok and he carried Rok because of his great size and weight" Brig said gruffly.

Jillian looked at Brig and could feel the weight of his pain. Oru was Brig's bondling and his friend. Moreover Oru had saved Jillian's life twice and Rok's once. How is he repaid; by being torn asunder by a idiot. Brig had a big heart and felt responsible for all of it. Even Jillian thought Brig in blind anger was going to kill Jar; she had never seen him come so close to loosing himself to his inner wolf. Jillian told Kerra as Jar was taken away to get medical attention.

"To start a war with Brigand Sawyer is to know defeat, but harm a friend or love one of his and you have sealed your fate, only death will save you from him, he will not stop EVER until he destroys you. Remember this Kerra, tread very carefully where Brig is concerned. His sense of honor is not pliable" Jillian explained in a serious tone.

"Jamis, you sent for us. Why" Jillian asked?

"I will answer that later. How did you break the link between Miko's G-jen and him, I had thought it impossible Korin" Jamis said?

The green eyed Guardian looked as though he were reflecting on the events of the combat, which to tell the truth was extremely short and finite. Then he looked at Brig and Jillian before he spoke.

"I inserted my own energy under his skin and ripped outward under the G-jen. I basically super imposed my energy flow over his so that he could not control the power of his gauntlet, It was the G-jen that killed him to be exact" Korin explained. "Moreover, Miko made an attempt on my charges lives twice, he has many times jeopardized the Guardians credibility, Therefore, I handled him as a threat in the only way I could see to stop him from killing Jillian. I whole heartedly doubt he could have beaten Brig, so the coward attacks his mate instead."

Jillian wanted to say that it was not like that, but she could not. Miko was determined to kill them. He saw them as a blight that he was compelled to cleanse. Jillian wanted to go home so terribly bad, it was her one wish. She didn't know if she would ever see her home again. Brig was one of them now, a Guardian and subject to their rules if she was not mistaken. It would of-course change nothing, if Brig decide to leave, they better make it happen or be willing to pay the piper. Brigand Sawyer was a soft heart, but when the wolf that lived in his soul was let out only Jillian was safe from his terrible justice. Jar had learned that lesson well. It also did not go without note among the guardian corps. Korin still baffled her, so strong and true, and semi-crazy, but there was a loving heart in Korin and duty that had shown through. Korin had killed another guardian for the sake of her safety. Why?

"Brigand, you have shown a mastery of your G-jen that I have never seen before. So perfect are you for the gauntlet you wear on your arm, that I don't believe you could be killed or parted from it, although I see you have put up a barrier around your arm." Jamis said.

"I witnessed how Korin snuffed out Miko and can't let that happen to me. If I did Jillian would be un-protected, I wont allow that ever." Brig said without looking up.

"I would have you stand before the counsel and the Guardians while I deliver my decision about you and your peoples futures. Would you consent to this Brigand Sawyer knowing it could go against you" Jamis asked?

"Yes, I agree. Know this old man, if any harm at all comes to Jillian at all I will annihilate your people and your world without mercy, starting with you" Brig said looking somberly right at Jamis.

"So be it. Korin, will you also stand with them; since you seemed to have tossed your lot in with these children?" Jamis inquired.

"Yes master I will, no matter what; I am with them." Korin told the speaker.

The counsel hall was full beyond the standard capacity. The Kylr people packed in to see the alien who whipped Jar and befriended the odd Korin.

The counsel came in and sat in their appointed chairs. Jamis as the speaker and head of the counsel sat in the center. The counsel looked distressed. One of the counsel stood suddenly and pointed at Brig, Jillian and Korin.

"Detain them" he said.

Several guardians moved and set to work a furious effort to trap the three persons standing center stage. Yet, nothing happened. Well, that is until Korin had enough of the theatric and slapped them away with a wave of his tiny hands.

"Get on with it Jamis" Korin said in disgust while looking at the counsel member who had over stepped his authority.

Jamis smiled and then chuckled. The elder speaker stood, and then turned and looked at his hapless friend on the counsel, shook his head chuckled again, then looked right at Brig.

"Brigand Sawyer what would you do for the love of your world. No, wait. What would you do for the love and companionship of Jillian, the human standing there holding your arm?" Jamis asked?

The boiling earth born man was about to speak, but Jamis held up a hand as if to say not yet son, not yet.

"Korin of the Kylr Guardians, reaper among your peers. Hero of the universe, my own trusted pupil, what would you do for the love of your world and that of your new friends on Earth" Jamis asked whimsically?

"Whatever I believe is required, to assure their safety and that of the Kylr and the universe I swore to protect" Korin replied dutifully.

"Do you love them enough to abandon your post and commission Korin, and if so to what end" Jamis asked?

The green eyed guardian began to follow his old master's line of thought and decided to follow along and help strengthen his cause.

"I love them as I have never loved another. Their lives will always be put before my own. Their welfare and future will be mine own adventure. They are, as close to being Kylr as I myself am. We are compatible both in body and in mind. I take them as my own." Korin said rather loudly.

The Speaker just smiled. Korin had understood him and was performing his role beautifully. Brig looked confused and Jillian was looking at Korin as if she could read the rebels mind. If she or Brig found out the truth of Korin, it would shock them to their core.

"Jillian of Earth do you accept Korin into your heart and as co-protector" Jamis asked?

Jillian looked at Brig, leaned forward kissed him on the lips. She turned her head and looked at Korin, then held his hand and kissed his cheek.

"Yes, I accept Korin into my heart and as an additional champion, a girl can't have to many defenders." Jillian said.

"Korin has been true to his word and has shown me unexpected friendship. I could not think of a better partner out here in the wilds of the universe where I am not educated in its ways. I except Korin as well." Brig said.

"Very well, it is my decision and that of this counsel that you remain in the service of the Kylr guard and Korin is to teach you the way. Korin will also explain a great deal more to you in private (chuckle). Jillian is in both of your protection and subject to your authority only." Jamis said. "It is also the wish of this counsel that the Planet Earth be protected and brought into the sisterhood with Kyl."

"I would speak Jamis" Said a portly fellow of middle years.

"Granted, the floor is yours" Jamis replied.

"I see no reason for such a lesser race to be afford the honor you purpose. What have they to offer us, they are primitive savages at best, and a huge nightmare at best" The portly man said without emotion?

"I would be very careful mister in your opinion of humanity, and if you want to know why we are so important to you, I will answer for the counsel. Babies, we are a fertile race and our genetic make up is nearly identical to yours in everyway. You might not think this is important, but if your people mix with mine your culture, your art, knowledge can thrive forever. If you choose to ignore that tiny important fact, you can take your might and glory to the grave" Brigand said with an edge to his voice.

"Are you going to expect the Kylr Guardians to protect your weakling race" The portly man asked?

(Snicker) "Your guard may be mighty, but in the common population, you arrogant bastards would fall to humanity like wheat before the scythe. We are among the strongest fighters pound for pound in the universe. If you do not want to lend us a hand fine, I will protect the Earth on my own, and GOD help anyone who comes looking for trouble, for I will be waiting" Brig said with a red tint in his eyes suddenly.

One of the gathered guardians took exception to Brigand's

speech and stepped forward with a word of challenge.

"Big words infant. You have just been granted a G-jen and you think that makes you powerful, it does not, the least of the Kylr guard could spank you without effort" A tall lanky Guardian spit.

"You are a fool" came a gravel voice from the doorway in the far corner of the hall.

All heads turned to see who the voice belonged to. A huge figure was lumbering along leaning on a massive cane. The new arrival's face was grim and set with the effort of walking in. He was in obvious distress, yet he walked with a straight backed dignity. The figure advanced until he was standing next to Korin .

"If you are foolish enough to challenge this one (pointing to Brig), you will be crushed like an insect no matter how powerful you believe yourself. This little human crushed Jar in less than a minute. JAR! Do you believe you are Jar's better in combat" Rok said?

The other guardian was at first confused and then it came to him that Jar had been beaten by an opponent. Suddenly he was weary of his decision to cross the human guard. Korin was smiling at him like he was a dolt. The Guard believed nothing human could not be the one who bested Jar, that simply could not be.

"Are you challenging him or perhaps not" Korin asked with a giggle. "It would appear to me that you have seen the futility of your assertion my silly man."

"There is no challenge, the human is unworthy of my efforts" The lanky Guardian said snide.

The fist of Korin's right hand was less than an inch from the lanky guards face when it hit Brig's left palm. The guard and the crowd gasped, for nobody had seen Korin move. Yet Brig stopped the blow dead the instant of impact. What that meant is, even though Korin moved first Brig beat him to the spot and saved his peers face.

"No friend Korin, it is not for you to defend my honor" Brig said smiling at Korin.

"I am beaten Brig. I was once the self proclaimed fastest Guardian in the Kylr guard and you bested my speed easily" Korin said amused.

"Not at all Korin, you just didn't think anyone would try to catch your move, so I am sure that was not your best speed to punch ratio" Brig said humorously. "Now about you smart mouth" Brig turned on the stunned guardian. "I am not going to let you off the hook. Attack me or I will flatten you where you stand."

Brig squared his shoulders and stood back rigid waiting for whatever was coming to him. The Guardian having witnessed Brig's blinding speed jumped right on Brig in a fury. The blasts and impacts of the blows were contained by Korin.

The onslaught was terrible to watch, unbelievable power was ripping into Brig who just stood there. He made no attempt to protect himself. His body was bleeding from everywhere. Korin's face usually so attractive was contorted with anger and fear. Korin could not fathom why Brig would not fight back. He was being cut to pieces by the guardian who was manic with the effort of trying to kill Brig; and yet, Brigand Sawyer absorbed all the punishment and utter not a single syllable. Jillian was crying and put her face into Korin's neck, because she could no longer stand to watch. Finally it was over, the guardian was panting covered in sweat. Brig was covered in blood. He spit a mouth full of blood on the floor and stood straight up and turned slowly, his eyes boring into the crowd.

"I stand here, STAND HERE, still after the brutal assault on me. I used none of my power to protect myself, I am ruined, yet for all his effort (He pointed at the exhaust Guardian), I am still upright. Earthlings are tough and resilient, you want to fight us, your weaklings compared to us. For all your advanced weapons and knowledge, you still nothing, because you have no heart" Brig growled as blood dripped out of his mouth. "Korin". The green eyed trickster dropped the barrier except around him and Jillian.

Brigand Sawyer taught the counsel and gathered Kylr to fear the hearts of man. He slammed his hands together and the building exploded. The walls and roof were annihilated. Not one single person was injured though. All who witnessed Brigand that day knew fear and learned a new definition for courage. In this mid sized human male they had seen a depth of honor and loyalty that was unknown outside of the Guardians of Kyl, nobody moved or spoke. Finally Jamis stood up and clapped, he was joined by every single Guardian on the planet, who all came when the building was exploded into dust. They got there and witnessed first hand that Brig had flexed without hurting anyone. They respected his show of restraint and power. Later when they learned of the assault he endured without defense they were in awe of him. This was the first day of a Bright new future for the Kyl, and it was brought to them by an alien, small but far from ordinary.

"I believe that Guardian Sawyer has proved his metal beyond at shadow of a doubt. Any who oppose his membership to the Guardian corps, needs to step forward and speak now or be silent forever more" Jamis said with authority.

"Any who oppose Brig, are mine enemy and I will fight" Rok said bluntly, on the verge of wrath.

"That goes triple for me, I will kill you, any of you if you ever attack Brig again, ever" Korin said sweetly, but there was no hint of a jest once 'o ever.

The Entire counsel held their breath, Rok and Korin were among the most devastating fighters within the Guardian ranks, Korin alone could likely wipe out half the corps in open combat, with Rok as well, it would be suicide to oppose Brig. There was only one voice and it came from Jillian.

"We did not come here for this, we were brought by Kerra and Jar, to help your people and ours. I am weak and frail by your standards, but Brig even before the G-jen was placed on his arm was a force of nature, I used call him the Wolf of the Winter, because he hunts alone, he asks for and expects nothing from anyone. If you are foolish enough to cross him or pursue me, your life is forfeit, he knows no mercy, because he has never been offered any. I ask you to accept us and our people as friends not adversaries, because if Brig makes war you will all die before he does" Jillian explained.

"She does not lie" came a voice from behind the counsel dais. Jar walked out into the day light and smiled at Kerra. "I foolishly injured his pet and he nearly killed me, if not for lovely Jillian, I have no doubt Brig would have lost himself in ire and I would have perished or been on the mend for a great long awhile" Jar explained.

The look on Brig's face was not a kind one, he was busted to pieces and still if it came to combat, his pain would not matter to him, he would go until there was nothing left of him to bring back. Korin walked over and put an arm around Brig and whispered in his ear, Brig nodded once and held out a hand to Jillian.

"I am going to take these two to my home if you require anything; but beware, come in peace or stay away, I also am not merciful by nature." Korin said with little humor. With a brilliant flash of jade they were gone.

"I ask you now Kyl do we live and thrive, or do we let pride and prejudice kill off our great people. If we do mix with our human cousins we can strengthen our hold on the universal peace and further our lives. We must decide now, you have seen Brigand Sawyer and Jillian his mate, can you find a fault or weakness in either of them?" Jar ask in an angry tone?

"Would you the Guardians of Kyl deny Brig brotherhood because he was not born here, he has endured great pain and injury to prove both his metal and resolve. I would not want him as an enemy, a force such as his, a burning spirit, a Bright light should not be turned away or dimmed because of fear, so I call for the vote, guardian or renegade" Rok asked?

The ramshackle room was silent for a long time. All of the G-jen lit up at the same time, and a thin guardian stepped forward and spoke.

"We are unanimous in our decision Rok" said Bello a group commander.

"What is the decision" Jar asked?

"Brotherhood" Bello answered with a smile. "One such as Brigand Sawyer is a natural for the mantle of Guardian. He will protect and never yield, Kerra has told all how Brig still carried Jillian after his body was dead, he willed it to moved, refused to face final death until he saved her. This is a man I will call brother proudly. I stand with Rok and Korin in defense of Brigand Sawyer, what say you guardians" Bello roared?

"Aye, we stand with Brigand Sawyer." was the united reply.

"I decree that Brigand Sawyer be granted the rank of deputy supreme commander to partner with Korin" Jamis proclaimed.

"I would like to be assigned to his service" Rok said?

Jar and Jamis considered this. It was not a good thing to have three major powers in one group but then again, Rok was clever and straight laced, knew the rules and procedures, and he may balanced Korin's temper. They agreed to the request. Thus the deadly trio was born.

"God help us all if those three decide to go rogue" Bello said.

"It would never happen, all three have a deep sense of honor and duty" Jamis stated.

"Permission to have the Guardians restore the dome Jar" Bello asked.

"Certainly Captain Bello" Jar said.

CHAPTER 7: KORIN.

In a misty grotto Jillian woke up laying on top of a hot rock covered in fur, to protect her body which she realized was naked. She was alone but extremely comfortable, she ran her hands over her sore body and was pleased at the firm muscles under her skin. She must hug her parents when she saw them again for the genetics gifts they passed along. She was tall, lean, had a small butt, and firm medium size round breast with small pert pink nipples. Brig loves to massage her all over. Where is he she thought?

The steam ridden air made Brig dizzy. He didn't know it but the steam had a special medicine in it that only Kerra and Korin knew about. It caused tissues to grow and regenerate at a super accelerated pace. Brig was warm and drunk, he hurt all over, but soft gentle hands were massaging him all over. He believed it was Jillian but when he rolled over it was a white haired girl, the steam prevented Brig from recognizing the girl. It was not Kerra, the breast were too small and muscular. They were nice breasts, good shape and placement on the body, however he had never saw them or the owner before. He tried to speak but they put a hand softly over his mouth and then replace it with their soft lips. Brig was loyal to Jillian but he was fuzzy minded and the person's body and lips felt right for some reason, so Brig for once did not want to fight it. They stayed that way for he did not know how long just enjoying the embrace. Brig thought, where is Jillian? He was just about ask, when the nude girl turned her back on him and he looked at her from behind, at her behind. She had a body very similar to Jillian's in structure; except skin, hair color and breast size was the only differences. She got up and melted into the steam. Brig was suddenly sleepy and alone.

"Wake up sleepy head" Korin said.

Brig sat up and looked at Korin. Korin seemed different but for the life of him Brig did not know why. Brig seemed to have a strange feeling that made no sense to him. Korin gave Brig a robe and left.

Jillian woke up with a soft body holding her close to it. One of their hands was caressing her belly and then her breasts. She was about to pull away when they kissed her neck just the way Brig does. Jillian pulled away just enough to face them. She found she was in the arms of a woman of just her build, she knew it was a girl because her breasts were pressed again the girls own breasts. Then suddenly the girls lips were on her own, and she did not want to pull away, Jillian was not a prude but she had never been drawn to girls, she was not against it mind you, she just never met a girl she wanted to be with enough to share with Brig. She was not jealous or greedy about Brig, she just wanted to keep their love affair private and between only them. Now, she was making out with an alien girl and she strangely really wanted to. Jillian lost herself in the moment, she ran her hands over the girls back and behind, and the girl rubbed her back as well. Jillian wanted to talk to her, but the girl put a finger to her lips and hushed her. After what seemed like to short of a time the girl disengaged from Jillian's lovely body and got up. Jillian noted what a tiny hard butt and fine legs she had before she was lost in the mist. Jillian fell asleep almost immediately after her girl left her sight.

"Hello baby, are you feeling better" Came the friendly voice of Korin.

Jillian sat up and looked at Korin, who was looking at her nude body with a distinct look of approval if not envy she thought. Envy, that makes no sense. Korin leaned down kissed Jillian on the lips and gave her a small robe, smiled and then rose to leave.

"You're a girl" Jillian said, it was not a question.

"I am the girl" Korin said. "How did you know Jillian"?

"I thought there was something about you when I met you. Your so protective of Brig, and your affectionate toward me, but not a like a man would be. Then there is your slim almost girl like figure when your fully dressed, you also have beautiful white-silver hair and Kylr men have no hair. I began to suspect you were a woman when you killed Miko, you could have over powered him but you didn't, you used you mind to beat him in a devious way like a woman would. Lastly, although you were careful not to let your G-jen touch my skin, I knew you had one because I have been able to feel you spirit since your skin touched mine, and then you could not resist kissing me" Jillian explain.

(Giggle)

"You are only the second person I have ever kissed Jillian, but I enjoyed your embrace more than I can explain" Korin said.

"Brig was the first, no" Jillian asked.

"Yes, but he does not know it was me. Please don't tell him. I think I am in love with both of you, I am kind of an outcast, so I don't think I could take rejection from him right now while I am so happy" Korin explained.

"I will keep my peace Korin, but sooner or later you have to tell him. If you leave him in the dark to long it will hurt you chances for lasting happiness" Jillian said.

Korin looked at Jillian with a forlorn expression.

"That is easy for you to say Jillian, you're a goddess, I'm a freak. Would you or Brig have paid me any attention if I had told you the truth about me? No, you would have been repulsed and I would still be alone and miserable" Korin said with eyes rimmed with tears.

Jillian went over to Korin and put her arms around her. They stood there leaning on each other for a long while then Jillian decided to speak.

"Korin, I knew there was something special about you, so does Brigand. He is bothered by you, because he feels the draw towards you and since he thinks you a guy, he is not sure what to do. Tell him the truth, show him yourself openly so you can be free of your silly notion that you're a freak. I think you're beautiful, I thought you were very sexy for a man, maybe to pretty. I thought at first you were gay" Jillian said.

"What does gay mean?" Korin asked.

"Gay means that you're a man that likes to have sex with other men, back on Earth" Jillian explained.

"Oh, I am a woman who loves both a man and a woman, what does that make me" Korin asked shyly?

"Blessed, because I think I can love you back. This is a single honor for you Korin, because until now I loved only Brig, and no other. Therefore, I will help you expose who you really are to Brig in a way it is impossible for him to refuse you." Jillian said with a Cheshire cat grin.

The girls got dressed and went out to find Brig and have something to eat. The hallway that lead to the grotto where Brig was sitting on a funny looking, yet comfortable chair was longer than Jillian would have thought. Brig got up and put his arms around Jillian. They hugged and whispered to each other as all lovers tend to do. Jillian said something in Brig's ear, then she bit his ear. Brig just smiled.

"Good Morning Korin." Brig said smiling and reached out and held Korin's left hand with his.

Korin took them down the hallway to some hidden stairs that lead up to a sunshine filled room that had a breath taking view. Jillian giggled as she looked out over Kyl and marveled at the different color variation, so different from her home planet. Brigand Sawyer being a country boy or mountain man if you will, saw a wide world that need to be explored and enjoyed. He smiled at his own thoughts. Korin served them a red-ish bread and some juice that was a cross between Strawberry and lemon, but very tasty indeed. Korin was a great hostess, she was witty and friendly and very clever in her views.

Moreover, Korin was pleasant and upbeat and not at all stuffy like Jar, or semi nasty like Kerra, although, Kerra is a gorgeous woman.

"Are feeling satisfied Brig" Korin asked him.

"Yes, great fare Korin, all quite tasty. Thanks" Brig said.

Jillian looked hard at Korin trying to encourage her to tell Brig about her secret. Korin looked crestfallen that Jillian would not tell Brig for her. Korin was just plain afraid of Brig's reaction to the news. Nevertheless, Korin decided to tell all of her secrets to these two all important people. Korin would risk it all for their love and acceptance..

"I want you to follow me to another room, with big fluffy chairs, that are so comfortable that you would likely fall asleep if it were not for our conversation" Korin said rising and walking toward a wall.

The white wall with a moon hand painted on it was where Korin went. She put her hand on the moon and hummed. The wall shimmered and a door appeared. Korin smiled and beckoned them to follow. Jillian took Brig's hand leading him into the room behind Korin. The room was unique to say the least. The fluffy chairs were there and they were red fluff balls. The floor was white and soft on their bare feet. The walls were a moving mural of unknown wild animals roaming the land. The floor to roof windows had the same landscape beyond.

"The windows are one way and damage proof; we are invisible from the outside. You are only the second and third persons to ever come here. I am alone and never bring anyone here, nobody even knows where it is located, and they never will. I am not a popular person among the Guardians. I am powerful and I am loyal, so when it comes to a fight I am desirable, yet only then." Korin said somberly.

"Well, you are a damn good fighter Korin, so that makes sense from that perspective. I personally like you, so the other stuff about being an undesirable outcast does not fit well with my view" Brig said to the utter pleasure of Korin.

"You know how I feel Korin." Jillian said.

Brig looked at Jillian and then Korin and his eyes narrowed dangerously. Jealousy was not something Brig had ever had an issue with, mostly because Jillian loved only him and he was hopelessly in love with her. Somehow Korin changed all of that. He was more possessive of her than even he knew. Jillian was happy because without Brig she was unprotected and helpless, he was her adored Knight in shining armor. Jillian believed that deep down Brig was fighting himself over Korin, the jealousy was likely due to the fact he wanted Korin as well, but did not know that she was a she.

"I do know. (Korin smiled at Jillian) I want to tell you a long story, so please let me tell you all of it before you say anything. I don't think I could get the courage to tell it to again, this is very hard for me because almost nobody knows what I am going to tell you. I was not born, I was made. Kerra for all purposes is my mother. She used her genius of science to create me in her lab. Jar for what it is worth is my father. It was the two of them who gave the DNA that made me. I am twenty three of your Earth years old, I am also the only progeny that lived" Korin said sadly.

"Go on Korin, we will listen to all of it" Jillian said.

The lean Guardian with slit green eyes seemed to take great pains to compose herself, finally Korin reached a level of calmness required to continue.

"I don't know about where you come from, but if you are different among the Kyir, you have no place, no friends, no life and no love. All the Kyir people as you have seen for yourself are fit and very attractive, perfect in everyway. I am not blue eyed and perfect like them so I am mate-less and lover free in a society that needs to couple as much as they can just to product offspring. Kerra, being the my mother (snicker), tried to arrange a coupling for scientific reasons but it seems I am undesirable,

therefore no takers even with a bribe from Kerra who is among
the most desirable of all Kylr females" Korin explained.

Jillian was gently sobbing with her face against Brig's chest.
Brig patted her back and held her. Strangely, Brigand wanted to
hold Korin as well, but he resisted because he did not want to
console another man in that way. Still, he could no deny how he
felt, which troubled Brig greatly. He was not sure that these
people had not messed with his mind or changed his personality.

"Please continue Korin" Brig said softly.

The Guardian nodded and then went on.

"I grew up alone except for my private teacher and Kerra. I never
got along with Jar, he beat me when I was young for not obeying
him. He has many other children with Kerra, but they were made
the old fashion way. None of his children would speak to me
unless they wanted to gang up and beat me down. I never fought
back, not even once until, they were picking on another little
child in the play zone. They had the kid down and were kicking
him, there was blood on their shoes but they would not stop. Out
of the five of Jar's children only one was a girl, the other four
were big boys and mean. I had three of the group down with
serious wounds and the other two were taking more damage
than I was, simply put I went berserk. I never fought before,
because I had no desire to live little alone fight about it. I beat all
five of Jar's brood, who were all at the least 30 pounds bigger
than me and a foot taller. Yet, I put them all down hard and kept
them down until they were begging for mercy. I did not give any
quarter because they gave none to Rok. Yes, the little boy was a
five year old Rok, who grew into a giant of a man. Later, Jar had
me summoned. Kerra had asked me where all the cuts, bruises
and broken bones had come from. I explained in detail the entire
ordeal, she contacted Rok's family and the story they told
matched mine. Jar did not care about any of that, he told me I
was to be beaten for daring to harm one of his precious children.
I laughed in his face and told him that I was one of his kids, and
if he ever placed a hand on me again I would kill him. Well, he
beat me pretty badly and I spent two months in Kerra's bed

healing. On the day mother told me I was well enough to leave, I took her magic scalpel which can cut anything with me. I went looking for Jar, when I found him he was in a meeting with the Guardians, so I waited." Korin said as she got up to walk around.

"What a bastard, I don't feel guilty about kicking in his teeth." Brig said.

The sun was mid sky and Korin stood looking at the world silently for a long time. It was hard to relive this part of her life. The pain she had endured was almost overwhelming to her even now. She took a big breath and turned her face was as fierce as any wild animal Brig had ever ran off his ranch. Brig who had a strong heart almost shivered at the feral anger in Korin's face.

"Jar knew I was waiting for him, and he thought he knew what I was about to do or try; but he made a huge mistake. I was not alone, I didn't know this at the time. I attacked Jar with the scalpel and he used his G-jen on me. He would have killed me where I stood, but another Guardian blocked his power and contained his gauntlet so it was useless. I cut Jar's throat and the tendon on the inside of his knees. He went down hard and laid there looking at me as I advanced on him. Jar is no coward, but I was so fast and insane he could not stop me or even get a hand on me. I cut him up pretty bad, but did not take his life. The speaker of the counsel ordered Kerra not to heal Jar for what he had done to me as a just punishment. Jar healed up and the power of his G-jen was restored by my silent protector. Jar never crossed me again. I told him publicly, next time he would beg for death. Jar learned to fear me that day. He was furious when a G-jen was found on my arm when I was fifteen, and not just a normal one but the second most powerful one ever made. I am almost without a rival in combat, I hate fighting, but I have nothing else. I become one of the most fear Guardians in the galaxy before my eighteenth birthday, sadly all I want is to be loved and that was never given to me" Korin said with tears on her face.

"Can I ask you a few questions now or is there more" Brig said?

"There is a little more that I must tell you but, I could use some conversation to help get the bile out of my mouth. I love Kerra, for all her faults she has been good to me. Jar I despise and I love him at the same time; because he is my father." Korin said.

"Was Jamis your teacher, and if so don't you think it was he who put Jar in his place" Brig asked? "Moreover, why did Jar make you his assistant commander, if you hate each other so much"?

"Yes, Jamis was indeed my Master in all things, perhaps he helped me with Jar who can say. As for my commission in the Guard to my level, I am the best, I have a record of excellence second to none, and the counsel saw to my appointment, even Jar had to admit my worth in the position" Korin said.

"Your worth is not easily measured I think" Jillian Said softly.

Korin blushed. Brig was confused again by the reaction and interaction between Korin and Jillian. Brig knew there was something he was missing. And so he was.

"What about Rok, he is a big guy now, did you become friends." Brig asked.

"Rok and I are not close but we respect each other and we have served as partners on many missions. He was closet thing I had to a friend before you two came here. Now on to the last bit of information I have to share" Korin said as she began to shake.

   Korin walked over to where Brig and Jillian were and started to remove her clothes. Brig was startled and started to say something but Jillian stopped him from doing anything by whispering in his ear to wait for it. Korin stood there in the buff, silver hair hanging over her breasts and Brigand Sawyer had mixed emotions.

"You are a lovely woman Korin and I accept you into my heart" Jillian said with affection.

"This explains a lot, your playfulness, protective nature, and the girl in the mist was you, right" Brig said with an odd look on his face.

"Yes, I am sorry that was me, I just wanted to hold you without being rejected at least once" Korin said with tears running down her pretty face.

Brigand Sawyer reached up and pulled Korin down into his arms and held her close, he looked at Jillian who kissed Korin on the back of her neck. They stayed like that until Korin stopped sobbing.

"You could have told us you were a girl; I was confused about you from the start. Every time you go near me my heart started pumping. Only Jillian has that affect on me. Since, I thought you were just a girl-ish guy, I arrived at the conclusion that this G-jen thing was messing with my mind. Now, let me tell you something; piss on the rest of the Kylr if they can't see how hot and sexy you really are. If Jillian does not mind, I think I want to love you Korin." Brig said.

"I don't mind, I have feelings for Korin as well, she wants both of us in the worst way, I think we have both been sexually attracted to her the entire time. I pushed away because you're the only man for me Brig, but as a woman and an exotic blue skinned one at that, Korin makes me look forward to the days and night the three of us will spend together" Jillian said with a flourish. "Besides, you promised Kerra you would try to have a child with a Kylr, and Kerra wants to see if Korin can make babies, in this way by accepting Korin into our heart and bed, you are fulfilling all of the standing goals."

Korin and Brig looked at a smiling Jillian.

"You are a mad genius Jilly." Brig said.

"You would let Brig have a child with me" Korin said with red rimmed green misty eyes?

"You're our baby now, we want you in every way. You and I are

Brigand's mates together we will raise the babies that we make together as a family" Jillian said as she leaned forward and kissed Korin softly on the lips.

"We might as well start now. Korin where do you sleep, no wait, let's go back to the grotto and make love in the mist. I like it there" Brig said as he ran his hands over Korin's back and her breasts.

The three of them stayed in a knot of bodies all the rest of the day. Jillian and Brig had been lovers for a long time, so they knew what to do to make the other person happy. With Korin now a permanent member of their love life the got to explore new things. Jillian got to enjoy a woman's touch and soft lips.

Brig got another lover with a finely tuned body who was madly in love with him. Korin finally received the love that she had dreamed about, and it came from another planet. They were so passionate in there love making that all three were lost in the fantasy that was their new life. Korin was not very good at pleasuring her new lovers, because she did not even know how to pleasure herself, Jillian gave her a stout biology lesson on both female bodies and function and males as well. There was lots of laughter and joy all around. It all came so freely between them. Korin decided that she like oral pleasures because everyone got a equal share and it had the same affect on all of them.

The days drifted by and joy lived in the hearts of the three happy people who lived in the mountains. Korin finally showed them the normal way of coming and going since Jillian could not just Shift to where ever she wanted to be, unlike Brig and Korin who could. Not all guardians could do it, but they could. The air outside was warm and crisp. The path led back down the mountain to a near Kylr city, they walked there for sport. The trek took them over and hour. The Kylr looked at Brig and Jillian intensely. Jillian was a popular spectacle, because of her beauty. Brig was pretty much the same as guys goes. Most of the Kylr kept their distance because of Korin, who had a reputation as a notorious thumper.

An over zealous man came up to Jillian and began to feel her up, which is common among the Kylr who are a very openly sexual society, because of the low birth rate. Jillian started to kick him in the nuts but Korin stopped her by walking up and putting her arm around Jillian and kissing her on the lips. The man withdrew fast. Korin and Jillian walked hand in hand around the city. Brig already was well known and many of the women made offers of pleasure for the chance to have his baby. Brig just told them it was up to Korin and Jillian, which basically caused the subject to drop.

On the way back to the grotto layer of Korin and family, Korin stopped and put her hand on Jillian's arm and there was a little pain and a jolt of energy. Korin told Brig to do the same. Brig complied. Jillian asked what that was?

"It is for your protection dearest. There is no such thing as rape on Kyl, we are open to any form of procreation that does not kill us. What we did, is we marked you as off limits, because you're pregnant." Korin explained. "The penalty for touching a Woman who is with child is very severe."

"How does it protect me, I am not pregnant" Jillian said?

"If you are approached by a male wishing to mate with you, you will give off a red and green glow, which will scare the crap out of them, because that means you carry a guardian's child." Korin snickered.

"Korin are you going to let the rest of the Guardians know you're a woman now that you have me and Brig." Jillian asked.

"No, I cant. It is against the law for a woman to be a guardian, I would be killed if I was found out." Korin said.

"I would never allow that now, Your mine and Jillian's, if they go after you I will protect you with every thing I got" Brig said seriously.

"I am not helpless lover, I would not role over. Most of them are afraid of me anyway. They think I am nuts, maybe I am" Korin giggled

"Wait a moment, if it is against the law, how did you get a G-jen and become a Guardian? Who placed the gauntlet on you" Jillian asked.

"Jamis" was Korin's only answer.

CHAPTER 8: FIRST ASSIGNMENT.

In the months that followed, Korin taught Brig the ways of the Guardians, the laws, the procedures. They bonded to a point of a scalpel. So close were they that they could almost think the same thoughts. Jamis not wanting to let the dangerous trio sit for to long sent for Rok and directed him to gather Brig and Korin for a mission.

Brigand Sawyer woke up between Jillian and Korin. He had his head lying on Korin's buff bare chest just below her breasts. Brig loved her more deeply than he thought he could. Brigand's relationship with Jillian, if anything was even stronger than ever before. Blessed, is how he felt everyday. The fact that he was billions of miles from Earth meant nothing because Jillian was with him and he had found a new love in the form of Korin. She made him complete in a new crazy way. Korin understood what drove Brig better than even Jillian did.

A buzzing noise made Korin's eyes open. She put a hand on Brig's face and caressed it. With her other hand she caressed Jillian's sleeping form. Korin smiled a deeply satisfied smile and let out a breath after stretching a little.

"We are summoned Brigand to the Counsel, we must go immediately" Korin said.

"What no time for love" Brig said with a grin.

Korin smiled Brightly and put a leg over Brig's ribs. The shift woke Jillian.

"I think that morning sex rules" Jillian said with a sly little smile.

One hour later Rok stood waiting in counsel for the two wild guards to show up.

There was a pop and green mist, from it came Jillian, Brig and

Korin. They were all smiling and touching. They were happy plainly. The gathered assembly of the counsel and Guardians were not sure if they should speak and interrupt the trio, even though they were all there to discuss a mission and the situation that caused the meeting in the first place. Korin was laughing about something until she looked at Jamis, who usually had a smile on his handsome face. He did not have a smile now.

"Brig, Korin and Ms. Jillian, welcome. Please sit down so we can get to the topic that brought us all here in the first place," Jamis said calmly.

The entire room had a seat while the speaker of all the Kylr people prepared his explanation for the group. Jar was present and so was Bello, both looked tense. Jamis finally was ready to proceed, so he stepped forward to indicate it was time to begin.

"My friends we have a serious threat to the peace and continuity once again from the Pirz. They have decided that with their new weapons technology that they can ignore the Guardians and invade the Grot home world. The danger here; as some of you know is that the Grot, who are a warrior race will defend themselves and a terrible war will start, once ignited to war the Grot will not back down, neither will the Pirz. What say you Guardians, how is this to be handled. We have tried diplomacy and it failed with both races" Jamis explained.

There were more than a few shocked or strangled faces among the guardians. They were the strongest race among the old powerful races in the universe, however, the Pirz weaponry was second to none, and they had no qualms about its use either. This was a serious issue, the Grot were friendly to the Kylr race but only the Kylr, any other race was just fodder to them. The Pirz were arrogant to the extreme, thus being as such, they like to force their will on other so called lesser races. The Grot were a insane choice.

"Who are the Pirz?" Jillian asked

"Silence woman, you have no voice here?" A buff Guardian said.

The mouthy Guardian did not even know what happened before he hit the ground hard. He bounced twice and slammed into the wall behind the assembled seating area. In a blink Bello was standing over him, with a look of pure malice on his face.

"Have the Guardians degenerated into arrogant trash, where a simple query is greeted with bile and evil. Where has you honor and self discipline gone" Bello spoke very softly yet all heard him plain as day.

"I thought to teach the female alien her place" The bruised Guardian said plainly.

Bello shook his head at the foolish man. What the Guard had missed was the fire in the eyes of Jar, Rok, Korin and the murder in Brig's own orbs. Bello saved the fools life.

"It is not for you or anyone else to teach Ms Jillian anything, she is the, excuse my expression the property of Brig and Korin, if you have issue with her then you may apply to them for correction. You are not to speak or touch her for any reason. The punishment for breaking this command will be final death" Bello said heartily, then looked around to include everyone in the room for effect.

"Well said Bello. Now, to answer Jillian's question. The Pirz are a human-like race, they have orange tinted skin, eye and hair color varies. The tell-tell sign they are Pirz is their eyes. They have slit eyes like a great Earth cat, which has uncommon night vision as a benefit. There is nothing else to tell you about their people. They are omnivores, they have various body styles, and two genders. There females are as fierce as the males in combat. Theirs is a military society, they have almost no arts or music" Jamis explained.

"Thank you Jamis for your explanation." Jillian replied.

Jar stood up and faced Brigand for the first time since Oru had been Injured and Brig had almost killed him. He regarded Korin with an obvious distaste, he turned to look at the giant Rok as if pleading for the large fellow to keep the other two in check. Rok looked right back at him with no hint of acknowledging Jar's thoughts or pleas. The supreme commander of the Guardians of Kyl was about to make history by sending Rok and company into action against the Pirz, he also named the group; a handle that they would always carry with them.

"It is the counsel's decision that the Terrible Trio deal with the Pirz threat. You three are to go to the Pirz home world and crush the insurrection before the galaxy is plunged into all out war. If you do not stop the surge on the Pirz home world, other races will join in until the entirety of their galaxy is fighting" Jar said in a flat tone.

Korin turned to Rok who was standing behind where Korin was sitting and then looked sideways at Brig with a twisted grin.

"Terrible trio" Korin crowed.

"Indeed" Rok added.

"I guess that is an apt name for us, it says don't mess with us, and we mean business when we come to town." Brig finished up.

Jamis watched the trio closely for any sign of unrest between them. There was none, all three seemed to be satisfied with their peers. If anything they seemed happy and confident, they spoke in an easy manner and joked about the irony of the situation. Jamis was pleased to see this, it would make them even more formidable as a force if they were untied in their efforts. Jamis worried about Jar though, he had never been beaten in combat before, and he would be dead if not for gentle Jillian's interference. Jar was a great man and an excellent officer. However, he was smarting about his status in the guard's eyes and his own as well.

"Do you except the mission" Jar asked?

"Yes" The trio said in unison, they looked at each other and laughed.

"Which one of you will lead the mission, and will the other two of you follow his orders to the letter" Jar asked looking directly at Korin?

"Korin will lead the mission, and we will follow. I have not enough experience, and Rok is not as aggressive as either Korin or I, therefore, since he is a more sedate warrior he will make an excellent back up and mission advisor" Brig said, turning to look at Rok. "That ok with you big guy."

"I am satisfied with your plan Brig" Rok Said in his deep voice.

   Jar looked physically ill for a moment, he recovered nicely but his paler did not go unnoticed by anyone. They thought Jar's reaction was a sign of disrespect for Brig who was dictating to an honored Guardsman, when Brig was not even a Kylr. They were in error, Jar did not want Korin to lead because Jar knew Korin to be a woman. Korin was Jar's daughter in name and D.N.A, however, Jar had no love at all for Korin. Frankly, Korin and Jar hated each-other with a passion. Jar because she was strong and meaner than him, as well as being a woman. Korin hated Jar because he failed to treat her like a person, he shunned her and abused her until she received her G-Jen, then he wisely backed off the green eyed nymph.

   Jamis had something on his mind but did not want to speak of it in general assembly. He listened as Korin outlined the battle plans and departure schedule with Jar and his companions. Jamis waited and watched them, and he watched the hungry eyes of the many Kylr males who watched Jillian closely. This was his main issue, any harm or violation that was visited on Jillian would bring Korin and worst yet Brigand Sawyer down on them like a veil of death. At the apex of the pivotal meeting when Bello agreed to lend air support to the trio, Jillian realized she was to be left on Kyl alone and she was scared. Jamis noticed her sudden revelation and decided to end the general meeting.

"Brig can you come into my private chambers and bring Jillian with you my son." Jamis asked?

They looked at the speaker with an edge of curiosity, followed him into the private chambers and closed the door behind them. Jamis sat down and turned to speak, he stopped looking directly at Korin. Korin smiled at Jamis, while holding Jillian's hand.

(Clearing throat) "Korin, I had thought to speak to Brig and Jillian alone" Jamis said.

It was not Korin but Jillian who answered the speaker, she smiled a sad smile and was white knuckled holding Korin's hand so tightly. Brig was silent, his mind was his own at the moment.

"Korin is our third, part of our family, what concerns us concerns her" Jillian said

"I see you have found out about Korin's little secret, it is for the best that you keep it to yourselves" Jamis said.

"It would be hard not to know, since we have spent months in her arms, bathed together, and practiced making babies. We have in a word pledge our love to her and her to both of us, for however long we shall live." Jillian explain to Jamis. "It is not that you did not know; you placed the G-jen on her arm yourself sir".

The speaker and leader of all the Kylr people was experiencing a new sensation, in all of his long years he had never known panic. The thought of Korin actually with a child and Brig's baby to boot, was a headache of planetary proportions. Being a diplomat Jamis did not show his worries on his face, instead he smiled.

"It may not be possible for Korin to be with child, she may be unable to carry one. Her physiology is not strictly speaking Kylr, and it is not human either. I don't want you children to be upset if it does not work out. You and Brig could always try to procreate with another natural born Kylr woman, the more the better" Jamis said gently.

The look of extreme displeasure found its way onto Brigand's face. Jillian looked appalled, Korin who was used to being pushed away had nearly no reaction passed a dirty look.

"Korin will be the only lover we take to our bed Jamis, we happen to lover her and she us. We have chosen, the decision is made and if Korin cannot have any kids so be it, she will still be our choice as a life companion. Is that understood" Brig asked with force.

The elder spokesman was taken back by the passion shown by all three. Jamis actually thought for a second Brig was going to strike him. How had love blossomed so fast and so deep between these young ones. Is this what it is to be a human? This passionate zest for life and loyalty towards a loved ones; these are the things Kerra said the Kylr needed to save them.

"My pardon, I meant no insult to any of you. I did not ask you back here to argue. I am worried about Jillian. When you leave to face the Pirz threat, Jillian will be unguarded. I trust nobody to protect her; she is a precious gem that everyone will want to pluck. Even, I am enchanted by her. We must decide how best to protect Jillian while you are off world on missions, since you and Korin will be together" Jamis told them.

The three of them had not thought about this, Brig was not happy and it showed. Korin looked miserable. They could not take her with them to a war zone, and they could not leave her here alone for God knows how long. Jillian was soldiering up, acting like it did not matter, she would be fine, but it was not so. Jamis offered no help, because he also was worried about Jillian, and he felt like a grandfather toward Korin, he loved the odd girl and did not want her to suffer or worry while in combat.

Brig was another matter. His insane affection for the girls, one of Earth and one from Kyl, if something happened to one or the other he would destroy the responsible party. Without Jillian, Brigand Sawyer may be the most dangerous man alive.

"What about Kerra, she is powerful enough to hold anyone who would want to try Jillian out" Korin said.

"Kerra want Jillian for herself and would try to experiment on her without her knowledge" Brig offered with a wry smile.

"She would not hurt Jillian and would not let anyone else touch her either under pain of death. Bello made that fact abundantly clear, publicly at the assembly. If we swear Kerra to protection only, then she will be committed to Jillian's defense, and any who crosses Kerra will rue the day they were born." Korin said.

Jillian made a funny face and looked hard at Korin. She did not seem to think from her expression, that Kerra was a good bet. In fact, Kerra was the most horny person either Brig or Jillian had met so far on Kyl. Her outrageous libido was a monster in and of itself, still Kerra was a brilliant mind as well as a gorgeous body, perhaps she was a decent choice after all.

"I will let you ask and make Kerra swear to no sample breeding with me, while you are away Korin. She is a very curious woman, she will want to dabble with my body to see if she can use what she learns to make the Kylr more fertile" Jillian said. "I am for helping your people, but not in that way".

The look on Brig face suddenly Brightened, he smiled in a way that only Korin and Jillian had ever seen before. He winked at both of the girls and turned to Jamis.

"I have decided what and who I am going to leave to protect my girl while we are off fighting" Brig said cheerfully.

The dry afternoon in the wastelands outside of the Kylr city, Kyl Prime, was a mist of hot roving the land, where there were very few trees to shade and cool the area. This was just where Brig wanted to be. He had not explained why he had come out here, not even to Jillian who knew Brig's mind and thoughts as well as even Brig did. She was baffled though. Brig just smiled and kept on walking until he was dead center of the violet grass covered expanse. Brigand Sawyer was not a person to chat for the sake of chatting, so he was silent. However, now that he was in the spot required by his needs, Brig whistled loudly in every direction.

"Oru, come I have need of you my friend" Brig bellowed into the wind, in each direction just to make sure.

The was a rumble when Brig bent down and placed the palm of his left hand on the ground and sent out a red shock wave. To any observer it looked like a mini nuclear blast wave. It was not meant to harm or destroy however, it only sent sound in a rolling motion to catch the Wira's attention. In the distance, there was a vague clatter and then the world went mad. The ground erupted and a giant furry snakoid shot into the air 25 feet above the two Earthlings and their Kyl lover. Brig began to step forward thinking this was his pet and Bondling Oru. He stopped dead as the ground turned dark and a huge bat creature dropped out of the sky on the snakoid. The snakoid opened its huge maw and snapped at the bat, but the bat had its claws securely into the Snakoid's throat. The snakoid could not escape so it rolled in on itself to trap the bat in the folds of its massive furry body. They two giants were on the ground wrestling for position, the snakoid was doing better than expected and the bat was bleeding from the bites. The Snakoid's razor sharp sword sized teeth ripped and tore at the bat. The Bat sank its dagger claws into as much of the Snakoid as was available and made good use of his own deadly teeth. The ground was soaked in the blood of both beasts, there were chucks of meat that had been ripped out of the Snakoid, and a few from the bat as well.

"Oh snap what am I supposed to do, which of them is Oru, is either" Brig cried in despair as one of these might be his friend!

The sudden blanket of green mist covered everything, and then crackled with power. Both giants took instant note of the unexpected interruption. Then they were frozen in place, unable to move at all.

"Which of you are Oru?" Korin asked?

"Oru save Breeg" The huge bat said,

"Oh shit I almost shot my own friend, I thought the snake was Oru because he was fuzzy, glad I decided to wait now" Brig said.

Korin released Oru from the energy net and gave the snakoid the opportunity to leave in peace or pieces. It made the right decision after the whipping Oru had provided him; it turned tail and went into the ground.

"You okay Oru, you took some damage" Brig asked with a genuine concern.

The Wira being a shape shifter, could change it's body around and become whatever is required to live or defend itself. It was currently seeping frank red blood from many bite marks. Worse, Oru seemed to be breath way to hard since he was the victor of the contest. Brig inspected the wounds and they smelled pungent. Brig did not even think about it, he looked around for a water source. There was a small damn a half mile away. Brig dropped to one knee and held out his G-jen encased arm and a red hot blast of raw energy ripped a 4 foot deep groove in the ground all the way to the water, the energy hit the damn at the base, the water spilled into the groove and ran freely to where Brig was on his knee and spilled over somewhat. Brig made a pond big enough to bath Oru in at the end of the groove and then shoved the big Wira bat into the water.

"I am not sure..."Korin started to say, then stopped because Brig yanked of his shirt and jeans and jumped into the water.

The water filled with blood and the poison from the snakoid. Brig begin to glow, he released his energy and let it flow around and into Oru. The water began to boil and Oru was screaming in pain and still Brig pour it on, more power and more energy. If the girls had touched the water they would have been electrocuted and burned. Oru was not the only one in pain Brig was suffering as well his skin was being boiled off and he was not breathing anymore.

"Korin save them, they are dying" Jillian screamed!

"I can't; I am not powerful enough to overcome Brig's G-jen, we have trust he knw what he was doing" Korin said with tears running down her thin face.

The horror of watching a loved one die is something I would spare you from if I could. Korin and Jillian however, were not spared from this, their hearts sank and despair set in. Never had Korin felt so helpless as she did at this moment. Jillian could not imagine life with out her Brig, she would not even think of it.

"ENOUGH" Brig screamed so loud that the girls jumps in fear.

The end on the pond was blasted down another twenty-five feet and the boiling water drained out. The damage to Brig was great and he was a mess. Tissue was not so neatly hanging off him, like loose threads do, not at all attractive to look upon. Oru was in even worse condition, but both were a live, at-least for now. Korin jumped down in the pond and ran toward Brig, he held up and hand forestalling her, Brig did not seem able to talk. He turned to Oru and place a hand on the Wira and said only one word.

"Revert" Brig said and then fell to his knees.

There was a morphing within the huge bat, his body shifted and bulged out and in. A terrible cry issued forth from his mouth. The bat gave way to a bald ape with tusks. The ape picked up Brig's broke body and carried him carefully out of the pond passed Korin. Brig was placed with extreme caution on the dry grass at Jillian's feet. Oru continued his transformation into the tiny monkey creature Jillian had first met, and then he too collapsed on the grass while touching the man who had saved his life for a second time.

Kerra was shocked top see the amount of damage that she witnessed when called to the med-center in Kyl Prime. Brig was laying on a table more dead than alive. The creature Oru the Wira was in even worse shape, yet both lived and it was beyond her how they could get so torn up and survive. Kerra at first thought about the possibility of a Guardian assault, but Bello, Rok and Korin would have slaughtered any foolish enough to try that.

"It was a Snakoid Kerra, it attacked Brig and Oru transformed and tossed it a beating, however, the little hero took several bites" Korin explained.

The look on Kerra's lovely goddess face was grim as she listened to Korin and Jillian explain the entire scenario to her. Kerra understood Brig's actions even though the girls did not. Still, Kerra feared that Brig's sacrifice was in vain. Nevertheless, Kerra was the best medical mind in the known universe and she loved Brigand Sawyer in her own off-beat way, and she loved Korin her daughter, Jillian was always in her heart as well. Kerra refused to let the veil take Brig.

"The Snakoid's bite is instant death, I have never known anything to survive it, yet Oru did. Brig boiled his friend to extract the poison from his body, Brig endured the same heat and pain so he could gauge the terminal point where Oru would die if he exceeded it. Both will need the finest anti-venom that I have, we must begin now" Kerra said

The Guardians were called quietly, Bello came and took Brig and company himself, not wanting anyone else to be trusted with Brig, and fearing Korin's terrible vengeance if any tried to harm Brig. Twenty hours passed and the hour for the departure for the mission was approaching and Brig was on his back. Oru was up and spent his time laying by Brig, singing a mournful song. Oru was so distraught that Kerra thought he may die of sadness if Brig did not wake up soon. Oru knew that it was his Breeg that had sacrifices his life to save Oru's. Wira were extremely rare and never friendly as far as the Kylr knew, yet Oru would protect and kill without as second thought for Brigand. The Iasomorph loved the small human so intensely it hurt Brig's friends to witness it. Only Korin, Kerra and Jillian were allowed near Brig, when anyone else approached the Wira transformed into a huge ape monster and just about killed them.

On the morning of the mission egress, Brig opened his

bloodshot eye's, scratched Oru on top on his still giant ape formed head, then sat up. Jillian noticed the pain in his eyes, but kept her peace.

"Oru I need you my friend, will you help me out buddy" Brig said in a deathly soft voice?

"Breeg Oru Breeg, I do eenything for you" Oru crooned.

"I must leave the planet to make war on my foes, I want you to protect and guard Jillian while I am gone, can I count on you" Brig asked his question

"Oru protect Jilly, no touchy, Oru promise Breeg, or Oru kill" Oru swore with passion.

"Please do as Jillian asks you and stay with her in our home hidden away from the rest of the world" Brig said weakly.

"Oru mind Jilly for Breeg" Oru promised.

The smile on Brig's face was a rainbow to Oru and the others gathered around Brig that morning. Jillian and Korin came forward to hold Brig in their warm embrace, covered him in tears and kisses. Bello did not understand why Korin acted this way but was wise not to ask.

"My gear, if you please girls" Brig asked?

"What your not fit to go anywhere especially to war" Kerra said.

"If I do not, your people will brand me a coward; who talks big and lets others die in his place. If that happened, then Earth will never be united with Kyl, and therefore will remain unprotected, I can't and will not allow that to happen to either of our worlds" Brig said with a hint of finality.

Three hours later Brig was dressed in the Kyl Guardian battle gear and he took a deep breath and stood up. He lean forward and held Jillian tightly in his strong arms and he trembled, not from physical pain, but from the pain of being apart from his heart and soul.

Oru hugged Brig and swore again to protect Jillian, loudly for all to hear and share. Nobody in their right mind would try the Wira after such a vow, only death could stop a Wira, and they were nigh impossible to kill. Therefore, Jillian was completely safe while Brig was away. Korin held Jillian so tight and whispered words of farewell and love. Korin turned away with tears in her green eyes and boarded the ship in one powerful bound. Brigand Sawyer bowed to Jamis and walked to the entrance of the ship, then turned and addressed the crowd.

"I will bring back victory, or they will bring back my lifeless body" Brig said and then saluted the Kylr people who cheered.

"That is the bravest man I have ever known, I would never wish to be his enemy," Bello said to Jamis.

The ship carrying Korin and Brig took off to fireworks and fan fare, Bello's ship followed closely and would do so for the next three standard months until they reach Pirz.

Jamis was extremely pleased with the turn of events. It was known to almost everyone among the Kyl Prime residence that Brig was on his death bed from fighting a Snakoid and he saved the Wira as well, moreover he refused to shirk his duty no matter what. Brigand Sawyer was fast becoming a hero to the people; not of his own home world, but of an alien race that were used to power and status. Jamis noticed that every step Brig took cost him greatly. There were many eyes in the crowd that were wet with tears. Brig asked for nothing and gave it all; yes we have much to learn of Honor and dedication from this man.

CHAPTER 9: PIRZ

The first night that Korin and Brigand were away, Jillian cried herself to sleep, as she would do every night until they returned. An ocean of tears fell for the trim young beauty, as her heart yearned for her absent lovers. Jillian's only joy was Oru who as it turned out was a great friend and companion. Jillian could go anywhere and was never bothered. Jillian had believed that she was to be a hermit until her babies returned, this was not the case. Oru dragged her out on the third day. They went to the cliffs were Oru became a great Dragon, with a soft furry back for Jillian to ride. Oru snatched up Jillian and flew around the planet unmolested. It became a normal part of the day for the Kylr to look up and see Jillian roaming the open skies of Kyl. Jillian was given the moniker **DRAGON LADY**, by the people to her adopted planet.

Jamis never stopped watching over both of them, he worried that if Jillian let down her guard for an instant and Oru had to save her, there would be blood spilled. Jillian's exotic beauty, skin color and bearing made her to rich of a prize to be simply ignored. Jamis decided that Jillian must be taught to defend herself, thus taking Brig and Korin's Wrath out of the equation. Oru needed nothing and was a fierce guardian, but somehow Jamis must convince the Wira to let him instruct Jillian in the defensive arts.

Kerra who had stolen both Jillian's eggs and Brig's seed, was quietly pregnant and she craved physical attention more than any woman had ever done before. It was like a drug to her. The normally stoic Jar was semi giddy with Kerra. Jar knew why Kerra was with child and would face down Sawyer upon his return about this personal violation of his trust.

(ELSEWHERE ON THE FLAG SHIP)

Korin watched Brig walked onto the ship a week ago and collapse into her bed in their shared quarters. Korin was worried in-spite of Brig's inner strength, he was so ill that only the fight in him denied the reaper his soul. This little man from a blue marble in space had stolen Korin's heart, and more important he returned her love, that was a pearl of great price all by itself. She was omnipresent by Brig's side, she slept with her bare skin on his, so that he could feel her warmth and love at all times. Rok made sure that they were left in peace, being a giant didn't hurt his chances of being obeyed.

Bello called Rok on the transship com.-link to ascertain the updated status of the man he was growing to admire. He was seriously concerned at the lack of information that Rok was able to provide. Korin would only say that Brig was asleep and in a bad way. Rok had heard Korin crying nearly everyday, he had not thought there was anything that could make the mighty Korin cry. He was wrong it both troubled him and encouraged him. Most people thought Korin was insane, Rok knew better, Korin was just bitter.

Bello decided as the senior member of the guard who was free to work, Korin was tied up nursing Brig, so it fell to Bello to take command of the mission. All of the seasoned Kyl troops trusted Bello's judgment and he was well liked, therefore there was no strife when he gave orders. Bello slept very little, and neither, it seemed did Rok. Korin slept in wisps only. When Bello could wait no more he transported over to Korin's flagship to inspect the situation with Brig and Korin. Bello walked down the corridor and nearly hit the wall. Bello was far passed exhaustion; he was on the verge of collapse. Moreover, all three of the other Guardians were in as bad or worse shape. Bello almost walked by a tall lean man when he saw the G-jen on his arm. Bello nearly fainted from the shock of it, this was Rok.

"What happened to you Man" Bello asked Rok?

"I sleep so little and eat even less, I am standing vigil for my friends, so that they can heal in peace," Rok said in his deep voice.

The door opened and Brig was standing there. His eyes were opened and red rimmed, his color was an ash white, there was a fine mist of perspiration all over him. Brig was clothed in only pant; that were basically pajama bottoms. Brig was so thin that all of his stomach muscles were like leather armor, and his veins were purple throbbing snakes below his translucent skin. Korin lay on the bed in nothing at all, with her back to them, so Bello did not notice her breasts.

"What can I do for you boys" Brig said.

"We require nothing, but your return to health my friend" Bello said warmly.

"You both look like shit" Brig said with a smile. He still looked like he was on the back side of his illness.

"Look who is talking Earth man: Rok said with a smile.

"Do you guys have any spirits on this tubs" Brig asked?

Both guardians just looked at him with a blank stare, they did not understand, Brig only smiled weakly.

"Whiskey, booze, a hard drink, alcohol" Brig asked?

"Yes, of course" Bello finally caught on." Come this way, Rok steady him" Bello asked.

"I can manage Rok, but thanks" Brig said.

Korin woke up and found that Brig was gone, so she hurled the door open and Rok was not there either. Korin went into a panic, thinking of all the ill treatment she had all her life. If they jumped him when he is so sick and damn me I slept through it, I will never forgive them, or let them live. Korin dressed quickly and ran down the corridors looking for any sign of Rok or Brig. In her haste she ran by the officers lounge where they were sitting. Korin almost cried when she backtracked and heard Brig's hoarse voice in the closed cabin lounge. Korin opened the hatch and entered, all three looked up at her as she sat next to Brig.

"I thought, well never mind that. How are you" Korin asked Brig?

"I will live. All three of you need to look to your own health, stop worrying about me, eat, sleep as needed. I apologize for not carrying my share of the load. I will not be a burden on you any longer" Brig said as he downed a mouthful of the green booze he was drinking.

"You drink much for a little person Brig" Rok said

"I generally don't drink at all, but I hurt all over and needed something to warm me up and dull the pain. Beside you all look like you needed a shot of the green stuff yourselves. What say we eat and then you people get some rest. I will man the bridge and take command while you rest" Brig said, more like an order than a request. The group was to worn down to care.

In the Officers dining room, four powerful Guardians ate together for the first time as a unit. They were only able to sample the fare because they had been eating so little that they could not hold a normal amount of food with the severally shrunken stomachs. Nonetheless, conversation was free and light and the assembled warriors got to know their companions better. All four of them left with a sense of who they were serving with and what that would entail.

The lights on the alert board next to the command chair where Brigand Sawyer sat were all blue or green, showing a non-hostile space, at the moment, not that many races would attack a Kyl ship, even during a war. Brig sat quietly and gave very few orders. The crew was plainly afraid of him. Any man that could live after a Snakoid had poisoned them was a god in their eyes. Brig, strictly speak was not bitten by the giant creature, but his Wira friend was, therefore Brig endure a bath filled with boiling

poison and energy to saver Oru. The effect on him was dire,
yet being a man of True grit as they say, he was not about to lie
down. A crewmember came up to Brig with a stylus.

"Can you check this and sign it sir?" The man said very politely
as he attempted to hand the stylus over.

Brig took it and looked at the readout on the miniature screen.
Brig had learned the Kyl language from Korin, so he could make
out the messages ok. The notes were actually for Bello, but the
commander was sleeping deeply for the first time on his own
ship in nearly two week. Brig was about to sign when he notice a
notation on the bottom. It said (If the Earth man or Korin step out
of bounds, trap or kill them to save the mission), it was signed
with Jar's seal.

"Sir, I beg your pardon, but you are shivering, may I give you this
blanket to warm you" Said a young man holding a blanket?

"Hell yes, I am not sure if it is that damned snake's venom or
Kerra's cure, that is worse" Brig said with a smile.

 Brig laughed for all the bridge crew. The crew burst into laughs,
because it was well know that the brilliant Kerra loved to dabble
and experiment a lot even on the ill.

    Brig made a mental note to tell Korin about the message from
Jar, and have her face Bello with it. Brig did not believe for a
moment that Bello was a back jumper or a coward, so if the deed
was to be done, He would be facing Bello like a man should when
it is important and unavoidable.

    The night and part of the next day waned before Brig could not
stand the pain and weakness anymore. He was startled when the
other two bridge officers came and helped him back to his
quarters, they knew how sick he was, and they showed loyalty
and admiration by helping him without being asked. Rok wanted
to take the next shift, but Brig said no, it was to be Korin, she
was not as tired or wasted away, so Rok was to rest and eat
again. Brig told the big fellow I need my team to be as strong as

they can get when it all come to a head on Pirz. The crew was surprised that Rok obeyed the order, but said nothing. Korin wanted to nuzzle Brig but was happy to let Rok rest since Brig was telling her to. Brig closed the door to his room and fell on the floor unconscious and there he stayed until Korin return sixteen hours later.

Two days passed and Brig took his turn at the bridge like the rest of the Guardians did. He paid a terrible price for being up out of bed. A fool could see the man was dying, but Brig's sense of duty and honor made the others leave it alone, therefore Brig stood the watch again and again without complaint. The crew came to respect and love Sawyer as one of their own. Brig's quiet strength and perseverance was the example all of the crew on the flag ship strove to imitate. Korin was in denial about Brig's pending death. It was a considered fact Brigand Sawyer's life was bleeding away and nothing seemed to stop the loss of the best man any Kylr how ever known. Most of the Kyl men decided that if this is what it was to be a human than they would be among the first to take a Earth woman as a lover and mate, not to save the race but to be part of it by extension, such was the level of adoration for Brigand.

(Back On Kyl).

It was a month and a half since her lovers left her on the planet alone with an alien monkey as her only protector and friend, that was then, this is now. Jillian was no longer so prim or proper, her lovely hair was clean, yet it hung down wild around her shoulders. She wore less clothing, it was little more than a bikini made of leather, her soft body was now harder, leaner and as wild as her hair. The look in her eyes was like animal that tolerates you and nothing more, it; if anything made Jillian even more beautiful and goddess like. Jillian had consented to learning the defense arts from Jamis, who as it turned out was a master with all the armed and unarmed forms. Jillian chose a weapon that looked like a blunt sword, it had a blue blade that was dull until the wielder became excited in combat then it was

razor sharp. The Bladed weapon weighed no more than a
single pound, so it was perfect for Jillian's smaller muscle mass.

Jamis was holding back in the beginning of Jillian's training
the first week, that was five weeks ago and if he held back now
she would kill him. It was like facing off with Brig or Korin, so
fierce was her onslaught that Jamis had to train her in seclusion
to stop any interference. Jillian was a wild exotic animal, lovely,
deadly. Her mind was sharp, so she made the choice to pour her
grieving heart into combat training, oh my GOD the passion this
child had in her, forgotten was the innocent child who needed a
protector, now Jillian was a 5'9 110lbs Amazon warrior woman.
Jillian was proficient with all the weapons he showed her, but
she was a natural with the Glave blade sword, it feed on the
users energy to produce the edge of the blade, the stronger the
wielder the more mighty it became. Jillian's blade could cut a
human hair down the shaft long ways into four, she had the most
deadly presentation Jamis had seen in his long life. Moreover,
she was the master of the blade with no equal, including himself.

"Well met, master Jamis" Jillian said as she pulled her weapon
than was slung between her shoulders.

"I don't believe that there is any use in crossing swords with you
Jillian, I can not match your skill and your speed in positively
inhuman. One would think you're a guardian with your abilities
child" Jamis said with a chuckle.

"Have you nothing to teach me now Jamis" Jillian asked?

"Just this" Jamis said as lightning-like energy jumped out at
Jillian.

The lightning was fast, but Jillian moved like a panther, fast
and easy to the side. Jillian brought her blade up, snapped it
down into the lightning so fast it was a blur of movement. The
blade cleaved the lightning and caused it to exploded back
toward Jamis, who moved equally fast.

"How is it your faster than men half your age, and you can toss lightning from your hands, it that magic?" Jillian asked.

(chuckle)

"No Jillian, I have my own secrets, I am a story that one day I will tell; for now child, I am impressed at your ability not to panic. I have never seen anyone who could more than stop the flame from biting them. You however managed to repel it completely." Jamis explained.

"I think of all the people I have met since my coming here, you are the only one who I would worry about if Brig had to fight them; Korin as well. You in specific are more powerful than Korin I believe, I may be wrong, but I sincerely doubt it" Jillian said with a deeply loving smile.

Jamis and Jillian had lunch on a shaded plateau above her home. Oru sat on her shoulder in his small monkey form. Jamis gave him bits of fruit. Jillian was wearing a short red mini dress. Her hair was braided over her right shoulder, and bound with a yellow ribbon. Jillian wore a smile that could melt the polar ice caps. Jamis thought to himself that she was truly the most beautiful woman who ever lived.

"Jamis, my parents are past now; they died a few years ago so; Brig is all I have now, him and Korin I mean. I am very fond of you Jamis, you are like a wise father, someone who knows what is to be done, and how to guide without smothering a person, Would you consent to being my adopted father?" Jillian asked the elder Kylr.

The shocked look on Jamis's face was near comical. It was impossible to guess at Jamis's age, he could pass for 45 or 100, the Kylr people do not age, because of near perfect genetic make up, therefore, he did not look old; well, he looked ancient sometimes and younger, much younger others; however only his eyes gave away any hint of age. In Jamis's eyes were a thousand life times of knowledge and wisdom. He seemed to be looking for the right words to say in answer. Jillian could not believe how shaken he seemed at that moment.

"Do you know how the Kylr feel about children, no of-course you do not. Once we were just like the people of Earth, we had mates that we swore to, and couples raised their children and life was good. Sometime, in our past there was a great sickness that killed a great deal of our children and most of our population. At that time our medical people came up with a cure, but the cure had a side effect, it caused our race to have fewer births every year. Therefore, we change as a people, coupling with as many partners as possible to enhance our chances of racial survival. This practice in the beginning was distasteful to us, because we are a proud and loyal people. It hurt us to have to share our loved ones with others; but if we did not, we would not be here today. Kerra is my daughter Jillian" Jamis told her.

"I didn't know" Jillian said.

"Yes, I have had many children over the years, and one or two were Guardians, most have passed on now. I am very proud of all of them. All of my off-spring were dedicated to the protection and betterment of our people, not one bad apple. I love children and they are sacred to my people, because they are rare. Kerra is my youngest child, I have not had a mate since I loved her mother. I am special in that all my children were with one mother, when she died, so died my desire to procreate" Jamis explained.

"Are you not lonely" Jillian asked.

"Sometimes I guess I am" Jamis said with a faraway look on his face as if he was remembering past moments. "Jillian, I would be honored to be your adopted father, it is a singular privilege not often granted or offered."

The Wira looked on with an orb sized eye carefully following Jamis just incase he did something Oru would need to beat on him for. Jillian sat and looked out over the terrain and smiled. She was at the moment feeling a sensation of deep contentment, Jillian did not want to even think about her loves who were far and away from here presently, because that would ruin her resolve to be strong.

(ON THE SHIPS)

The two and a half months about the Kyl flag ship was a new exciting experience for Brig who was dying slowly, the only thing that kept him from the veil was his iron will to live and the G-Jen on his arm. Guardians were immune to disease, but he was poisoned by a deadly predator's spew.

Bello walked the corridors of his ship, and searched the archives for a way to save his friend. Kylr physiology was just enough different, that the anti-venom Kerra had given Brig was not effective enough to save him. This small alien had the respect of every member of the task force and won the right by deeds to give commands to all of them. This was a new dawn for the Guard, a new zeal, courage, honor, it had all returned in the form of Brigand Sawyer. Damn it all they were loosing the spark of greatness to the veil. Bello could not allow this, he would save Brig, and there must be a way.

Korin stood looking out the port window to the stars. No matter how many times Korin had been in space she still loved the exotic black beauty, that were the heavens. This day though, she found no wonder, she saw no beauty, her soul was on fire, her reason for living was dying. Korin had never in the past understood how hollow her life had been. In the few months that Brig and sweat Jillian had been on Kyl, they had changed her life and her soul. Korin could not go back to what she was, even if she died in battle that would be better than to die of a despairing heart, and burnt soul. Brig must live, not even Jillian was enough to keep her going, and she loved Jillian more than her next breath. Korin stood her watch and Rok's because she feared to sleep. Brig may die if I am asleep, she thought, so I can not sleep.

Rok had taken up a human habit since coming on this mission with Brig. The small human had introduced the giant to reading books. Brig taught the Guardsman to read English and then provided him with some fantasy books that Kerra had appropriated when she was studying Earth.

Rok was in heaven, never had he used his imagination before, he found he was good at it and it made him feel important, this new skill. Rok sat with his book on his lap thinking not of adventure but of his friends, for all his massive strength and resolve, he could not do a damn thing to save the most influential person he had ever known. Rok would offer to take Brig's place and die for him if it were possible. Rok was sorely depressed.

In the gang way off the side of the bridge, Brig was teaching the crew to pitch pennies. It is a simple and old game, that anyone can learn and win at. At the beginning the crew thought the game was lame, and that was until Brig tossed a penny and made it lean perfectly against the bulkhead. Then it was on, all the crew in turn tried to come close or better Brig's toss. They failed. The game went on for hours, and nobody thought it lame or a waste of time, it was fun and skill orientated so they played hard to win. Even ill Brig was the master toss artist, the junior deck officer was second best with his gentle pitches. The crew wondered at Brigand's merry making, they knew his pain was insane and his death was near yet this man acted as if it was just another day. Brig actually seemed happy. The junior officer finally asked the question all wanted to know the answer to.

"You have made no arrangements for your departure, you do not seem like a dying man sir, don't you care about it, are you not scared" he asked Brig?

(Weak laugh)

"I am screwed son, I am not long for this life, I have made my peace with the fact I am not going to survive my illness. I am proud to have served with heroes such as you, good strong men and women with justice in their hearts. I can go to my reward with only small regrets my heart, my lovers will be lost without me to comfort them, I am ashamed of my inability to be there for them, but alas it is in God's all mighty hands now boys" Brig said softly.

The crew cried to the man right there and then. They had never known such courage, and they felt helpless in the light of this great man's demise. Brig showed no fear of death, not a single hint of weakness. For a powerful race like the Kylr, it was still very uncommon valor. The junior officer spoke then and shocked Brig.

"I will take your place on the ground if you die before we arrive, I will take my own life so that you G-jen could be placed upon my arm, so that your spirit will fight with you friends and their back will be covered, it give you my word, if you will allow to" Junior said

"If I die, you may do just that if it is Korin's wish, for as our mission leader and my loved one; it falls to her to choose since I will be dead and have no say" Brig said honored at the offer.

The junior officer Milo became the ships captain that very day, his courage and loyalty were rewarded by the crew and Guardians alike. Bello called the ship to attention and waited while Brig walked out in front of the assembled crew.

"We will be at Pirz orbit in a week or so, and this ship must fight and support the ground troops, when the guardians leave the ship you will have to act on your own. I am very proud therefore to promote one of you to the position of captain, and that man will be in absolute command of this vessel, he will answer to only the Guardians on this mission. Will Milo please step forward" Brig said.

Everyone waited, Milo hesitated unsure if he was being called or if it was indeed another person. Korin walked over and took his arm and pulled him over in front of Brig, who pinned on the new rank of his position as skipper of the flag ship.

"Congrads Milo, you're the man I want at my back when the fighting starts" Brig said.

Milo newly ranked was confused, he had believed that he was to be taking Brig's place in the ground assault force. Brig seeing Milo and the crew's distress explained.

"I am dying, DYING! Milo, I am not, I repeat NOT going to my reward on my back like an old used up whore. I am going to stand up and I am going to fight with every God given breath I have left until the Pirz put my face in the dirt. I promised you all this, (Brig turned to look at all of the rows of Kylr) I will not go gently into that good night, I will fight like these Pirz have never seen, once again the universe will know why they fear the night and the Kyl Guardians. Too long have we shown mercy and restraint, no more, I am dying, therefore I have nothing more to give than this lesson, which I will teach the enemy. You make swear off my actions later politically as if I was a renegade outcast" Brig growled so fiercely that many took a step away from him.

Only Korin was unmoved, physically anyway. She stood with tears in her emerald eyes falling not for agony, but for pride in her friend and lover.

"Aye, we shall teach these war loving trash a harsh lesson by a strict master, I am with you Brigand Sawyer, I name you my brother publicly, if you should fall I will annihilate the Pirz in vengeance" Bello proclaimed with a deep conviction.

"I will not leave the planet if you fall my friend, or if Korin our sister should fall I will fight until I am dead or they are all defeated" Rok said in his baritone voice.

"Sister" Bello asked?

All eyes w suddenly were on Korin, and she did not flinch or even take the offensive. She made no more to defend herself, she did nothing. Bello came to stand in front of Korin, he looked into her lovely eyes and reached out and lifted her arm with the G-jen on it. He shook his handsome head, trying to understand what he just heard.

"Well, care to explain any of this Korin" Bello asked carefully.

The air was buzzing with energy, none of it came from Korin. She refused to rise to the occasion. Rok however, was glowing like a neutrino star. Brig put a hand on his massive arm and shook his head no. It was against the law for a woman to be a Guardian, but it was also against the law for a non-Kylr to be one also. The law was foolish since Kyl women fought along side the male members of the race equally. Brig decided it was time to change the law, so he laid down the law.

"Release my lover Bello, and all of you listen to me well. I am not a Kylr, yet I wear likely the most powerful G-jen ever made, Korin wears its twin I believe. Korin has served your race as a guardian for years and it peerless in combat and warfare. Does the fact that she is a girl matter? Does the fact she was made by Jar and Kerra in Kerra's lab matter, they are still her parents? Would you question the judgment of Jamis who place the G-jen on Korin's arm? Well, would you? If Korin decides to fight you can any of you defeat her, well can you, can anyone?" Brig said?

"It matters not, I have known Korin since we were but children, she protected me when I was once a small boy, and helpless. Her sacrifice was made in blood. I knew then Korin was a girl, and I kept silent all these years out of respect for the best guardian I have ever known, until I met Brig. Korin is my sister by my choice and I will defend her if she will not defend herself." Rok Snarled as he came up to look down at Bello who was a foot or more smaller.

"Calm Rok, easy does it my friend. I have never known anyone except Jillian who deserved love and respect more, and that is just because I have known Jill longer. Korin has an inner fire that if she let it out unrestricted, the universe would both experience the greatest joy and the deepest terror. Korin has my love, respect and my protection. I have enough power to enforce my will, I will not however. Korin has more than earned the right to wear her G-jen openly as a woman, she has served long enough, showed she is the best of the best, she took all the suicide missions to save her brothers from certain death, because she cared" Brig explained as his eyes turned to a solid glowing red.

Milo pushed back the other crew and soldiers, like a captain should to protect them. Bello just looked at Brig and Rok. Korin did nothing, she waited to see where this was all going. Bello was making a life decision, for himself and for Korin he seemed to understand. Milo looked as scared as a man could be that his new command was about to be in ruins, and the crew lost. Bello stepped away turned his back on Rok and Brig. The only one who could like take Korin in a fight was with her in everyway, no room for mistakes on Bello's part.

"I agree" Bello said at length.

"What" Rok Boomed?

The Guardian commander turned and smiled at Rok, walked up to Korin, stopped then put his arms around her in a firm hug. Korin was shocked. Hell, so was all the crew, except Brig. Bello turned to Rok and addressed him directly.

"I proclaimed Brig my brother, and you proclaimed Korin your sister publicly. Korin is Brigand's lover and mate, therefore family. Family should never fight among themselves. Moreover, I have admired Korin for as long as I have known her, I was strangely drawn to her, now I know why. Korin is a girl, no, sorry a woman" Bello stated with a smile. "Besides the law needed to be broken, Korin is, as Brig stated the best of us, I stand with you no matter the risk or the law."

"As do we all" Milo said.

"So be it, done and done." Brig said letting his power flow harmlessly away.

They Guardians all dined with Captain Milo in his cabin that evening. Korin showed up in a very sexy dress, with her silver tresses pulled back into an elaborated set of braids. The dress left most of Korin's long legs bare up to the back of her thighs.

Her slender feet were also bare. Korin wore a small gem around her neck, a gift from Rok. When Korin arrived, even Brig was bowled over by the sight of her. Bello gasped. Rok giggled.

"Welcome to dinner my lady" Milo said elegantly.

"Thank you Milo" Korin said lightly with a pretty smile.

The men just gawked at Korin. She had never had this quality of attention except from her lovers. It was obvious to Korin that her transformation was well received. Simply put, Korin was breath taking, stunning in form and fit. Her silver mini-dress played to her natural beauty that she had hid all her life, but no longer concealed it.

"My God Korin, your look amazing. If I didn't know you were the same person because of your G-jen, I would assume we had never met" Bello said with a silly lustful grin.

"Thank you for the necklace Rok, it is lovely" Korin said.

"It is a tiny bloom on the flower of your overall beauty, my tiny sister" Rok said happily.

The dinner was excellent and the conversation stayed light and friendly. Milo was well suited to running the ship it seemed; and it was not only the new goddess among them who seemed to have blossomed.

Late that night Korin slipped out of her lovely party dress, put her little gem necklace in a box, and cuddled up to Brig. From somewhere down deep Brig found a great amount of energy, which he used to love Korin as passionately as anyone ever could. Korin gave it all she had as well, since this would likely be the last time they ever coupled, she wished Jillian was there to make it perfect, as it turned out, it was outstanding. Brigand really out did himself, Korin was shaking at the end from exhaustion. Brig held her tightly and she could feel his heart pounding against her breast. Brig fell into a coma like sleep. Korin cried and nuzzled her mate, wishing that she could have had a baby with this man, and a long life with him as well.

CHAPTER 10: FEAR BRIGAND

The captain and crew of the Kyl flag ship were all battle ready two days before the arrival in Pirz space. As a war loving race the Pirz were at a constant state of ready to fight, they were alert and ruthless, therefore Bello and Korin and encouraged the captains of each ship to be ready far before the orbit of Pirz proper.

Brig had slept every since he had mauled Korin in the sack. Korin made her peace with the fact she would never see his eyes again opened and looking at her. She thought to herself, at-least he got to see me as a woman openly in a dress once. Brig slept silently, he did not move or toss. If he did not snore or the rise and fall of his chest was not present you would think he was dead. Brig's temperature was through the roof, Korin had the ships Doctor give Brig something to keep the temperature down, but nothing worked.

Finally, the Kyl Guard reached Pirz space. There were hundreds of ships set around the planet waiting for them or anybody else who came to play. Milo and Korin had talked about this and were in no way surprised by the show of force by the Pirz. Bello and his ships captain were equally ready for the showdown, since both of them were seasoned vets of many campaigns.

Rok was mustering the ground assault forces and getting them squared away near the drop craft, or shuttles if you like. Rok kept looking at the hatchway, the crew knew it was Brig he was looking for. The ship started rocking back and forth, because it was taking on fire from the Pirz fleet.

"Bello have your captain strafe the down the port side of their fleet, we will take the rest" Korin said into her headset.

"Roger that Korin" Bello said.

   The scout ship was an instant blur of motion, Pirz ships were being ripped to shreds. Just so you know, Kyl ships have level 9 shielding (1 is weak, and 10 is all mighty God level) and level 7 weapons. Pirz ships have level 5 shielding and level 8 guns, a stupid combo by a thinking race.

   Therefore, the Kylr took the fight to the Pirz with a vengeance, too fast was the Kyl scout ship to even have it's shields tested. Every other Pirz ship was totaled in a blink of an eye. The heavens were littered with parts of ships, dead bodies and other refuge. Bello's ship never slowed or stopped flipping and somersaulting to and fro, with every move another Pirz ship was rent apart.

   Korin was just finishing dressing Brig in his Guardian battle armor, which could withstand a point blank blast from a pulse rifle (A weapon that shoots a short burst of a laser beam), bladed weapons or lesser projectiles. Korin had dressed Brig because she intended in taking him on the mission live or dead to honor his wishes to die in services and not on a bed. There was a pounding on the hatch that could only be Rok's giant fist. Korin hit the door release and Rok put his head through the door. He looked down at Brig fully armored and gave Korin a quizzical look.

"Bring him" Korin said as she picked up her gloves.

"He is more dead than alive Korin" Rok more asked than said?

"He comes" Korin said as her green fire ignited around her armor.

"As you say lil' sister" Rok answered.

   They made their way to the drop craft,; while Rok carried Brig like a baby in his massive muscle corded arms. Korin snapped a few harsh orders to the soldiers and they all got on the craft.

"Saddle up boys, let's rock" Korin said with a twisted knowing smile, because this is what Brig would have said. "Milo, get ready to drop the bucket".

"Roger that Korin, give'em hell for me" Milo answered.

"Take them down Milo, don't let them shoot our asses off when we jump." Korin said.

"God speed My lady, come back to us" Milo said sadly. He knew very well this was a suicide mission, almost all guardian missions were. They did not send in the Guard until the diplomats gave up.

   The drop craft popped out of the Flagship like a new born baby, and grabbed traction as the engines fired, it shot through the wreckage like a wasp through a rose garden. The pilot was a young Kylr girl with the reflexes of a prize fighter, she dipped and bobbed around everything with no emotion, she only spoke one word as they ripped into the atmosphere.

"Ready" the pilot said on the com.

   The hatch on the craft popped open, drop crafts never land on the ground, they drop the soldier and Guard and get back to their parent craft for the next assignment. The soldiers got up and locked their weapons into full auto mode, Rok stood at the head of the line, Korin took the rear guard slot, that way the soldier could be shielded by the guardians as they fell to the planet surface and not be killed. There was an unexpected burst of crimson light and it went through the door. Korin's head ripped around to where Brig had been strapped and he was not there.

""GET OUT OF THE WAY" Korin Screamed as she bulled through the soldiers like wheat to the scythe!

"EEEEEENNNNAAAAAAWCHA" The Guardian screamed as the corona grew around them to a small star.

   Rok jumped out the door in a huge orange sun burst, he pulled out several soldier with him. Rok wanted to blast the gun turret but the red avenger was mangling everything below and around him. The soldiers and Rok had gravity shoots to slow their fall, Korin did as well. Brig was using his G-jen to blast himself around as he seen fit. The Pirz were shelling the shit out of him but he slapped them away like gnats. And his retribution was terrible to behold, he flattened buildings, turn entire companies of soldiers to ash, and fell like a comet toward the ground.

Korin who was called the destroyer by her enemies, was terrified that her and all her Kyl soldiers would be murdered in Brig's rage. Brig said he was determined to go out with his boots on, and by GOD he meant it. Korin had never known fear, no this was terror, before. Brig hit the ground like a canon ball, leaving a 50 foot deep crater. He came out of the ground like a wild mystical dragon bent on destroying everything. Brig was beyond speaking, he was running completely on autopilot. The Pirz shock troopers tried everything to stop Brig, nothing worked. Brigand Sawyer, who all the Kyl loved seemed to be no more, in his place walked a monster.

"Rok shield our troops from Brig" Korin ordered.

"My God Korin, what are we going to do, Brig has lost his wits and he is destroying the planet around us" Rok said in a shaky voice.

"We support him, and follow and do a sweep and clean up, so keep moving and watch you necks" Korin commanded.

The was an explosion right behind Korin's troops, several of them were killed. Korin was fine, a guardian in full combat mode is nigh invulnerable. Korin jerked around in a deft movement she superimposed herself in front of the living members of her force. A beam of incredible force nailed her in her stomach, throwing her like a leaf in the wind. Korin landed just behind Brig. What happened next made the history books.

With a roar much like an Earth lion; Brig dropped to his left knee, he slammed his glowing hand together and screamed again in the direction of the beam that hit Korin. A beam of even more force came right out of Brig's mouth, it went harmlessly by the

Kylr troops and level fifty city block flat and smoldering. Brig reach over and took the head set off Korin's head,

"Milo, lock on my position, walk it out 200 clicks to the north and fire storm it" Brig growled.

"Roger".

The flag ship tore the area in focus apart. Brig tossed a barrier around the troops and literally swooped them up dropping them beside Korin. Korin had the dust knocked out of her but she was alive and angry. Brig did not speak, he only squeezed her arm and went right back to work. Brig dropped the head set in Korin's lap and turned to leave.

"On your feet soldiers, were at Brig's back, kill anything that moves, no quarter" Korin snarled. She had been leery of letting her power go, that was before they hit her with a new powerful weapon. Korin found her teeth and claws, and the Pirz if any lived would regret it.

Bello was up to his eyes in Pirz ships, they were not the Kyl scouts equal in combat, but they were in the thousands to only his and the flag ships guns. Worse Milo was shelling the planet now; or so Bello was told. It was something about Brig's orders. Bello thought Brig had died already.

Rok confirmed in shaky tone that Brig was not dead yet, in fact he was a juggernaut ripping through the capital.

"Milo, that will do, we can take it from here" Korin said into the com.

A sudden report from the right rear of Brig sounded. Brig's right chest erupted and his own blood sprayed on his face. Before Brig could turn as fast as he was, Rok came out of nowhere, reached out with his ham sized hand and ripped part of the wall down, through it right into the sniper cutting his body in two. Rok went over and stomped the remains for good measure. Brig spit a mouth full of blood on the ground winked at Rok and walked on into the city with blood dripping from his chest and mouth.

The three enraged Guardians spread out in a V-formation, Brig in the front like an arrowhead, Korin on the right green flames burning the night away. Rok's Orange aura was on the left and the big guy was covered in blood, none of it his. He took some damage but not as much as Brig. The Pirz, fearless as they were, got the hint finally and hit the ground running for their lives.

The supports ships were getting a workout above the planet. The scout had some minor damage for lucky shots, but it still was raising hell for the Pirz who were sustaining heavy losses. It was not the speed of the Kyl scout, or the pilots that cause the Pirz to loose, no, it was their shield, they were weak, so their ships just went poof if they took a hit. Once again bad idea on their part, arrogance is a serious weakness, if your opponent is ready for you. Milo on the other hand being a much larger slower target took a good tapping. Some of the minor systems on the ship where flickering, but Milo trusted the crew to keep the bucket together until he could get his Guardians back on the ship and blow for Kyl.

"Put out the fire in the loading bay before the drop craft goes up" Milo shouted in the com.

"Check skipper we are on it already down here, it will be contained; Chief out."

On the other ship Bello was getting nervy, he was a guardian and should be on the ground helping the terrible three end this war fast. If the Damn Pirz were not such aggressive fools this would not be happening, more if he looses his brother or sister down there, well the planet will be forfeit, he vowed to himself. Yes, It would be a grave crime, planet-cide, but Bello was set and would not veer now.

The third day of the campaign found Brig standing on top of a hill looking out over the planet, it was burning as far as they eyes could see in any direction. Behind Brig stood Rok the giant guardian with a wild orange glow in his eyes, he had not spoken in a full day, not even to issue orders. Korin gasped in horror at what the three of them had achieved, not because she felt remorse, but because the sheer amount of death and destruction boggled her mind. She never in her wildest dream thought it possible to raze a city by hand in such a short time and Pirz was a giant planet.

"Men you get some rest" Korin said though she herself did not seem to be about to get any.

"We need to get the central counsel to end this foolishness, I am sure they are in the south heading away from us. We need to tone it down, so they don't know we are coming" Rok Said.

"No" Brig said.

"What, why not" Korin said "It seems to be the only way".

"Oh, I get it, Brig will raise some Kane in north and we will go quietly to the south. They will think that we are all still here and let down so we can catch them unawares" Rok said, "Brilliant".

(On Kyl)

The ambassador from Pirz was livid, he was informed that his planet was being crushed by the Guardians as he spoke. The great counsel from all the main systems was convened, they listened to his protest, but no more. The Pirz were warned not to mass for war against the Grot who were not well liked, because most races feared their hulking forms. Nevertheless, the Grot were blameless this time and if it came to war they would give as good as they got, tough and resilient was the Grot middle name. The Pirz made a heated speech about the right of his people to do as they wished. Jamis listened to him, but motioned to his old friend the reigning Prince of the Grot, who was the great grand son of the first supreme commander Elor, who came to Kyl for food, that he would speak next.

The Grot prince was an odd one for his race, not in form but in manner. Elon was a nice fellow, thoughtful and wise. His mind was one of the finest in the court or grand counsel. He was never quick to anger or yell, he preferred to beat his foes with his mind. Although, Elon was a powerful fighter, no thinking Grot would try him in combat, because all who had tried him were dead. Elon did not morn them, they served as a reminder that he was their master and would not be challenged.

"The chair calls upon Elon, the floor is yours Prince" Jamis said, cutting off the Pirz.

"Thank you speaker Jamis. I would like to ask that the counsel understand we hold no angst against the Pirz, we offer no threat or insult. They simply want to prove they are stronger that we are. We will not back away from any fight if we are pushed, we will crush the enemy. However, I ask the Pirz to lead away from this path, it will not bring the galaxy any comfort" Elon said.

Many of the gathered counsel members knew that Elon was acting more civilized than they would if it were their planet that was about to be attacked. However, some of the members secretly wanted the Grot destroyed. You see the Grot did not just beat you, if you lost the fight they ate you. It was barbaric, but the Grot had offered peace to all who left them be, if you crossed them they felt you deserved the consequences that befell you. Fair is fair after all.

Kerra was reading a report sent by Milo secretly. It was grave in content. It covered all of the illness to the best of his knowledge where Brigand Sawyer was concerned. It also spoke of new weapons that could penetrate the Guardians energy shell and injure them. That is why the Guardians were still on the planet after more than ten days. Half of the valley that held the Pirz capital was laid to waste by Brig alone. Nobody knew where Rok and Korin had gone, they were perhaps dead Milo's report said.

"Damn" Kerra said to herself. If she had known how ill Brig was she would have never let him go. Then again now maybe Jillian would consent to mate with Jar or another Kylr to produce new children.

Jillian was on Oru's back flying through the night sky, they were hunting snakoids, and Jillian knew that Brig was excessively ill because of the venom so she was intent on killing the giant predators. Jamis had told her that, they could find no reason they could not be eliminated, they were part of no food chain, they had no positive influence on the land either. They destroyed and killed, that is all they were good for. Jillian took up hunting them right after that. The giant snakoid would come out at night and wait for prey to wonder close enough to kill and eat. Jillian and Oru would ambush the snakoids and cut them to ribbon before they got away most of the time. A few got away, but they never learned, so in the end Jillian killed them.

Jar watched Jillian hunt the dangerous creatures from afar and was scared for her. One bite or even a drop of venom in open wound was fatal, Jar feared to let something happen to the girl. Jillian had become so wild, and she carried and used a Glave Bladed sword like a master, and she attacked like a lunatic, and always killed the beast in the end. Moreover, she sold they hides in the market for clothing, rugs, blankets or whatever. The people call her Dragon lady, and many feared her blade, others worshipped her strength and beauty. Jar was one of the later, he did not love her, he just wanted to mate with her. Jar was sure if he tried while Brig was gone, his death would be a given if Brig or Korin came back alive. Little did Jar know that if he tried Jillian, she herself would kill him.

(Above the Grot Home world)

A large ship with new stealth technology was scanning the Grot defenses for strengths and weaknesses. The Grot who are warriors, understand and fight only with honor did not have stealth tech, it was cowardly to them, therefore they did not suspect anything at all. If they knew there was a ship up there uninvited they would have blown it out of the sky, yet they did not know. If Elor the 2nd found out some race was casing his home, he would put them on the menu literally. He was not like his grandfather the first Elor, who was the greatest king the Grot ever had. The current king was blood-thirsty and mean, his only weakness or check and balances if you will, is Elon who was more powerful than him. Therefore the king not wanting to face his son in a death match, kept his bad temper and attacks on other races on the down low, so that Elon did not feel compelled to remove him from office.

CHAPTER 11: RESISTANCE

In small hamlet off the beating path Brig found a small cabin type structure, and since he was so very tired he decided to hold up and eat something. Brig had to let down on his energy out put or he would incinerate the food stuff he wanted to eat. He had to make sure he did not let his energy drop to low though or he would drop dead on the spot. His body was toast, he pushed himself beyond the limits of what his flesh and blood could endure. Why, he asked himself am I doing all this, what am I to gain. Survival for Earth was his answer. This was a larger burden than he deserved to carry. However, there was nobody else. Brig ate his food in silence and reflected on the life he had lead. He smiled at the memories. Special among them were the two days that changed the face of his life, the day he met Jillian, and the day he found out Korin was a girl. Brig thought how odd was the opinions others had about him. Brig was a small, shy guy, there was nothing about his that said anything other than not worth a second look, yet, others looked to him to make the big differences. How ironic that Brig felt himself cowardly, because he needed to be motivated by another person to get the courage to act. Nevertheless, others thought about Brig as if he were important, this baffled Brig, and Jillian's love for him had never made sense to him, but only death would keep them apart, how prophetic those thoughts were Brig chuckled, under the current circumstances.

The small band of Pirz fighters that were watching Brig, had trouble coming to grips with the reality of him versus the myth of this man. They kept a constant eye on him. Brig seemed to be a gentle spirit, not a killer. The leader of the band gave instruction about a watching schedule, so that nothing Brig did would go un-noticed by them. Most important, under no circumstances was anyone to approach or engage Brig the Guardian.

In the wee hours of the morning one young Pirz decide since Brig looked asleep it would be the best chance ever to kill him.

He quietly crawled over to where Brig lay in the cabin, put a gun to his head and pulled the trigger. The shot woke everyone up, including Brig. The guy who had shot him was crawling away. Brig jumped to his feet and seized him.

"OH MY GOD, your just a boy" Brig said in astonishment.

"Yes, he is" Said the leader.

The moment seemed frozen in time, no one moved, until the boy cried out in pain. The bullet intended for Brig's brain, bounced off Brig's shield and hit the boy in the stomach. Brig laid the boy down and ran a hand over his stomach; and he could feel the bullet in the kid. The boy looked into his eyes and Brig put a finger in the bullet hole and blasted the round to nothing, he used his energy to close the kid's wounds. The he stood up and walked over to his gear, where he stopped and packed it up. He stood again to leave and the Leader stopped him.

"Why did you save him" He asked?

"He is only a kid, and kids should not have to die because the adult can't get along, don't follow me anymore friend, I have no quarrel with you, only your government, but I am not merciful a second time" Brig said calmly.

"Wait, we are against the government as well, they take our young and brain wash them until they act like monsters and kill everything, we can help each other I am sure of it" The leader said in a rush.

"Why should I trust you, he tried to kill me and your Pirz" Brig said pragmatically.

"Those are good questions, we were told you were sent here to kill all of us resistance fighters, how can we trust you." The leader said?

Brig tapped the com on his neck and made a sour face. He looked at the freedom fighters and realized the horrific mistake he had made. He needed down deep to make this right for these people.

"Cease all fire immediately," Brig said into the com on his neck.

Two hours after a cease fire, Rok, Korin, Bello and Milo were gathering with Mart the leader of the Pirz freedom fighters. Mart explained the conditions that their people lived in. It was very illuminating for the Guardians, who were told all if the Pirz were fanatics about violence and war. These freedom fight types were passionate but they were not the enemy, their own government was. The freedom fighter came to understand that Brig and company were not their enemy either. More over as it turned strangely about the freedom fighter spoke for the people, they were heroes to the people because they stood up to the corrupt government.

A daring new game plan was hatched among the new congregation to bring down the despots in the ruling class that preyed on it's own population. Mart told Korin, who he was obviously smitten with that the freedom fighting bands need to be bought up to speed on the join operation between the Kyl and Pirz common folk, so that none of the good guys would get shot up by mistake. Korin and Mart disappeared for three days just after that, while Rok and Bello trained and mixed the Pirz with Kylr. Milo went back to his ship and gave the Pirz ships a good shellac, just to keep them honest. The ruling class hid like rabbits in a hole. Even the Pirz people were not sure where they were, but they were confident they would figure it out when the appoint hour came.

"Hey in the camp." came the familiar voice.

"Come on in Korin" Rok boomed.

"Why all the cloak and dagger, we have mini coms, you could have let us know you were coming a long way off" Bello said amused as well.

The lean female Guardian came in the camp minus Mart and

she was dirty head to toe. When she walked in the Pirz looked her over hard, because they were scared of the Guard's powers. Now with Mart not returning with Korin, mummers started. Korin noticed.

"Mart told me to tell all of you Zumi" Korin said with a dirty faced smile.

The Pirz all relaxed and went back to their preparations for the coming campaign. Rok and the resistance took to each other pretty quickly. The children followed him around fascinated by the man-giant, Rok seemed to really enjoy the kids and their little faces and millions of questions. Of all the Guardians who came to the Pirz, Rok was by far the most popular, Korin was fairly popular as well for her strength and wild good looks. Brigand Sawyer on the other hand was avoided like the plague, everyone was scared to death of him, and the reaper is what they called him. Mart had told all the freedom fighters that Brig was a honest man and his honor was beyond question, moreover the tiny human was dying which made him volatile and deadly. The exception to the rule was the kid that tried to kill Brig; he stayed close and learned a lot about guts, duty and a great deal about judgment. The kid watched and more important listened to everything Brig said and learned from him what it was to lead and sacrifice yourself for the people when needed. Brig didn't mind the kid and spoke directly to him when he thought he should explain things more completely, Matho was his name.

The Pirz ruling body had a spy in the freedom fighters who was informing on them. Mart knew and kept the person semi in the dark, that way his people didn't get killed. Mart was not around at the moment so Bello decided to single the fool out and let him learn a few things. That was until the ruling body decided to kill Brig. The spy crept up and began to watch and study Brig for a time and place to off him quietly. Brig was not aware of the spy but that did not mean that nobody noticed him watching Brig.

Korin and Bello shot off to do some recon with a group of Pirz fighters and Brig and Rok stayed behind to fix and rebuilt rifles and teach combat tactics to the untrained, but willing common folk. Matho watched the way the Guards took apart and cleaned, oiled and reassembled the weapons, in a swift way. Both Rok and Brig made minor improvements, like smoothing out the trigger mechanism so the gun would not jam on the user. Rok trued all the barrels and cut new sights for weapons without any to make it easier to hit what you aimed at.

Matho and the rest of the free common folk were in awe of the mighty guardians of Kyl, they were beyond explanation, there did not seem to be anything they could not figure out. For the first time in Pirz history the people could see a light in the tower of their deepest hopes. They could become a free people, and not in some distant time but now, thanks to these selfless aliens.

It was early morning and Brig walked the edge of the camp every night and every morning, he made it mandatory that one Guardian be awake to back up the Pirz common people in case of an assault. Brig pull most of the duty himself, he wanted to finish the government off as soon as he could, his life was running out, he was unsure how much longer he had to live.

The spy snuck up and was about to stab Brig in the back when a black clad figure attacked him like an insane Wira Monkey in heat. The spy was completely over matched by his attacker. The black clad figure opened up a can of whup-ass and poured it all on the spy. The spy slashed with his poison bladed knife and the black figure darted nimbly out of range and then darted back in with a harsh inside knee kick, follow by a palm strike to the nose, snapping the spy's head back violently. The spy hit the ground hard, but managed to roll and throw the knife accurately at the black figure. The instant the blade was about to sink home into the black figure Brig snapped a hand out and the knife went right through his palm. The black figure gasped understand at once, both their life was saved and Brig's was lost to the poisoned bladed.

"Foolish out-worlder, your dead now" Laughed the spy.

The spy only got to begin laughing before the black figure pulled a knife of their own and went to work on him. Blood ran from a thousand wounds and still the black figure was not satisfied. So complete and total was the black figures resolve not only to kill the spy but to have the spy beg for death, that mercy or a quick kill was out of the question. The spy tried to speak but received a slash across his vocal cords as a reminder there was to be no discussion in the matter. Finally as the spy was wobbling from blood loss did the black attack yank off his hood to reveal his face. It was Matho, the youths eye blazed with wrath. The spy died of surprise it would seem. When the deed was finally done, Matho sat and cried, not for the spy but for his new friend and teacher. Matho had fought like a lion, he was better than even he could have ever hoped to become already, now his mentor was no more.

"Well done Matho" Brig said.

The startled Matho jumped to his feet knife in hand, he relaxed when he saw Brig standing there. He watched as Brig just pulled the knife out of his hand and then the same hand began to heal as if by magic. Brig was not dead.

"How is it you're not dying Brig" Matho asked.

"I am dying, but not from this puny poison, I have snakoid poison in my blood stream, that is what is killing me Matho, the poison on the knife is less than useless against me, but you didn't know that. Therefore, my fine young friend you stepped up your attacks to a whole new level, I have trained you well, but you learned more than I taught I think" Brig explained.

"Korin, Rok and Bello showed me things as well. I had to learn so I could protect you from back attacks, I had to be powerful enough in combat that I could handle anything to keep you safe. I have walked in your shadow every night, watching for attacks, that is why I am in black" Matho told Brig.

"Well you are impressive Matho and I am honored that you find me worthy of risking your life, however I am dying already, so don't waste your precious days and years on me" Brig said sadly.

The human walked away into the dark to call out the patrol to burry the spy in the woods and rummage through his stuff for anything useful. They set to it immediately.

"Damn the kid can really fight" Rok said suddenly.

"Yup, he is natural, if he lives he will serve his people well" Brig said.

Bello returned and was told what happened to the spy, he was angry because he wanted to use the spy to set up the government with false info, but he kept his tongue when the people told him who killed the spy and why. Bello being a wise leader acknowledged the boys victory and moved to a new plan.

The following morning when Mart and Korin came back a counsel pow wow was set up and plans were set to end the conflict and depose the current ruling class. It had never been attempted before. Korin reported that Mart's sister is one of the cooks for the supreme counsel, she told Mart where the black hearts was hiding, along with the rest of the cowards in the Government. Therefore the plans were being set and the time to go was in the morning.

"Get some rest tonight people, tomorrow we fight for your freedom" Brig said.

Korin herded Brig off and laid down by him and held him tight, they did not speak. It had seemed like forever since they had a moment to be together. Korin nuzzled him, Brig squeezed her, until Korin fell off to sleep. Brig knew he would never see Jillian again so he concentrated on her image and spoke his final words of love.

(Back on Kyl)

Jillian's eye opened with tears in them, she could see Brig's face and hear his voice. (I love you and I always will, I don't think

I will make it back to Kyl alive, I will never be able to raise babies with you but I wanted to. Korin may loose her mind without your love to hold her together. Both of you need to move on and remember the love we shared and be happy).

Jillian cried so hard that Oru came over and held her head against his massive chest gently. (Breeg).

CHAPTER 12: BRING DOWN THE HOUSE.

In the twilight of the next day after the big rebel meeting Korin led the rebels into a quite little valley, where all the government were hiding. Rok and Bello went around to the opposite side of the valley, so they could hit the government from two sides and above. Brig asked Milo to shell the building from space to soften them up, when he gave the signal. More, Brig told all the guard not to use too much power, he suggested they keep it to gorilla warfare, tight and personal that way the collateral damage would stay to a minimum, it was agreed. Brig with Matho by his side would enter and take all the guards out, as soon Milo ceased fire, in this way the central guard for the ruling counsel would be caught with their pants down and unaware. Brig took Matho and a few others aside and fitted them with armor like his own, Milo delivered it to Brig the last time her was planet side.

"This stuff will make you harder to kill, I did not train you to see you gutted and dead on the floor, so wear the armor, make sure it is secure, and take no chances with the good life God has given you. Remember your freedom hangs in the balance if we fail" Brig said sternly.

"Then we will not fail" Matho said as he pulled his black cloak over his armor.

"Right. Here carry this" Brig said strapping a big knife to Matho's thigh, "This bad boy is unbreakable and can punch through steel".

Milo started pounding the valley hard and kept the assault up for twenty minutes then stopped as directed.

Brig moved into the side of the building away from the carnage, with his five commandos went silently into the underground fortress, they used small thin blades to slip under they jaw bone and up into the brain the way Brig taught them, the victims did not feel any pain, but they were quite dead, and all very quietly put to rest. Brig had hoped that the internal security would be offline as a result of the pounding from Milo, no such luck. A klaxon began to sound all through out the installation. Matho pulled his dark cloak around him and started shooting out the lights. Brig looked at him.

"We are better in the dark than them, I am evening the odds" Matho said to Brig as the other four guys grunted their agreement.

It was pitch dark, and noisy. It was just as Matho said, the rebels were better in the dark and with the racket from the klaxon, the central guard could not even hear them coming until it was way too late. Brig was fast realizing another serious problem, the underground base was monster sized and he could not find the central hub. It could take weeks fighting at this rate to smoke them out. Wait, that is it.

"Retreat, out, everyone back out of the base" Brig yelled with a devil grin. "Korin do not enter base, I repeat nobody enter base, instead fill the air intakes and open doors and hatches with brush and fuel it with paper trash and light it off, and keep the fires going until I say other wise" Brig said in a rush.

"Roger that Brig" came the baritone of Rok.

"Acknowledged" Korin answered.

"Affirmative Brigand" Bello stated.

The rebels found and planted fire in every possible local that clean air could get into the base. To witness the sight, you would think that the rebels were feeding a lava field, so hot was the entire area. It resembled a volcano. Brig kept Matho next to him, knowing the restless youth would dive into the building and attempt to slaughter the enemy alone if he had to. Brig's plan was brilliant in the cost of rebel lives, because it cost them none. The base rumbled as they tried to filter their air supply, but the shellac Milo put on them prior to Brig's min invasion ruined the air exchanger unit that were too near the surface to be well shielded. The Ruling body of Pirz never considered that they could be bombarded from space by a powerful race or just one that was really peeved, so they did not plan for it, that was the rebels good luck right there.

Milo reported that the Pirz ships were turning planet side, and suggested that the ground crew hide. Korin gave the order and everyone went to ground. Forty-two ships landed around the base, because there was nothing they could do from the air, so they decide to help the base manually. Strangely enough being in the midst of a war zone was not enough to encourage the captains of the Pirz ships to guard their ships as each one became empty of crew.

"Can you believe that bullshit, did they really want to invade the Grot? It would have ended in a big dinner if you follow me" Whispered Rok. "Hey Brig, Korin asked permission to blow up the ship."

"Why not, once they are clear nuke 'em" Korin said to coin one of Brig's earth slang.

The air command of the ships, literally walked away from open starships unguarded and tried to put out the fires. Rok waited to get the crews about five hundred yards away then he stood up and blasted all of the ships to oblivion. The rebels captured the crews who were mostly unarmed, Korin was appalled at how easy this seemed, where was the intelligence in this action, they seemed like children playing solider, not real soldiers.

"I wonder if they have had enough of us, we have been putting the boot to them since we made orbit, and we thrashed the country side as well. Perhaps there is no fight left in these dogs" Brig said.

"Perhaps not, pretty stupid mistakes on the whole" Korin agreed.

There was a huge blast in the sky and it did not come from the surface, like an anti air battery would have. The is no ship that the Kylr knew of that that pack such a punch. Some of the prisoners were chuckling. Matho got angry and snatch one of the Pirz crew up at the point of his deadly blade.

"What is so funny brother" Matho said as blood began to run down the man's neck?

"Matho chill" Bello said. "There is another way kid"?

The young rebel smiled and stepped away from the prisoner with a twisted smile. The boy liked Bello, the guard was an elegant mix of tact and force. Bello stepped forward and looked the sneering man in the face, Bello smile sweetly as the prisoner realize the danger a tad too late.

"Burn" Bello said as the air around the man turned to a blue hell of licking flames.

(Screams of anguish)

"I want to know what the blast was, or I will cook you to death slowly. Your choice sir, I would not presume to order you around" Bello said in a soft gentle voice. Only the guards eyes gave away the deeper malice.

(Insane screams of pain)!

"Pulsar on the third moon, rail gun on the second moon, please stop" The man screamed.

"Milo you get all of that" Bello asked?

"Roger that noise. Our scout ship is gone and all hands aboard her. I will level the batteries in the next few minute or die trying" Milo said in a growl. He took the loss of his comrades and friend badly.

"Good hunting son" Rok said.

"Yes sir, thank you" Milo said and then he was gone.

The night sky lite up like the fourth of July as Milo and the flag ship ripped the 3rd moon apart literally. He was mad, too mad to care about loosing the fight. Milo had learned a great deal about protecting and operating his ship. Wise was he in the art of saving his craft, but not this time, he intended in driving it right down the enemy's throat, and all the crew were with him in this plan.

Fifteen minutes into the battle there was a nuclear explosion in the sky, all of the Kylr held their breath hoping it was not Milo's ship and their ride home. The atmosphere was burning the falling debris. It was not a ship that was falling, that was obvious when the firework began again. The second moon being smaller and more vulnerable went up like a lit match.

"Take some this; you bushwhacking sons a bitches!" Milo snarled into the uni-com.

The men on the second moon knew they were lost and despaired.

Milo blasted the moon from the opposite side from the rail-gun, so they could not even shoot at the Kyl ship as the moon was blow out from under them. Milo had taken both of the guns out and lived to tell the story. He would go into the history books as one of the greatest captain who ever lived and his victory would be a thing of legend; and Milo deserved it.

The falling moon bit skipped on the atmosphere and was really very pretty to watch, a few hours later it stopped and darkness settled in more profound than usual since two of the moons were destroyed light could not be reflected off them in the night sky. The crew and captured soldiers were complaining that they were hungry, Mart laughed at them.

"Can you believe these guys, they are hungry. Well our children and women have been starving, raped or murdered for generations, you can eat your own hands for all we care dog" Mart said loudly to a wave of approval.

"We did not decide these things we are only soldiers" a man said roughly.

"True but you carried out the beatings and rapes, murders, you burned our home and people. Therefore, you get nothing until the ruling counsel surrenders" Mart said for all the rebels to hear.

"They will not give in to scum like you" the man said.

"You better hope they do or your about to starve to death brother" Mart said in a flat dry tone.

Rok had enough of waiting, he powered up until it was hard to look at him, so Bright orange that it hurt to look at. The giant turned into a mole (not literally), he tore the ground apart and ripped through the metal reinforce bunker roof and started straight down. Bello fell in right behind him using his energy to incinerate anything that was loose so there could be no cave in on top of them. Korin and Brig made to follow but Bello held them off with a raised hand.

"We need you two out here protecting our back, you're more powerful than we are so we need you to mount a sturdy defense until we can smoke out these scum. Matho, your with us kid, we will need your stealthy skills no doubt" Bello said to Brig.

"So be it, we got yer back boys, go get the bad guys, and Matho, we want a few alive please" Brig said with a smile at the youth.

The ground shook and quaked for three days, as Rok tore the base apart literally. He was like a big blue wrecking ball, covered in orange sauce. Bello spent a quiet vigil behind Rok cleaning up any strays, and any runners that looked dangerous got the extreme displeasure of meeting Matho and his blades in the dark tunnels, for the first and last time.

Milo had his hands full on the ship. It was severely damaged and the propulsion systems were dicey. Milo personally worked around the clock to fix the problem. It was his ship, and he did not want the Guardians to think him unworthy of the post and promotion he was granted. If he only knew how profoundly proud they were of him and his crew in the past conflict, his show of courage and ingenuity in the face of overwhelming odds set him apart as an officer and a man. Nevertheless, for all his hard work, the damnable engines were messed up and may or not be able to push the star drive to a high enough velocity to jump into hyperspace. The main problem was that the power conduit was so fried that it was unusable, there was no spare. Milo thought about parts from the scout but there was nothing left to salvage.

(On Pirz)

Mart proved to be a very fine diplomat, he rounded up the people, organized them. He deputized a police force, set the farmers to work again and provide support. Mart inspected the bakery and fresh vegetable supplies and made scheduled for the masses to be fed. Mart seemed to be the favorite to run the government and the planet. He appeared to be popular with everyone and respected even by the prisoners. He worked tirelessly to assure that what must be done to continue to live was done first, then prioritized what was left.

The days went by in a blur as the rebuilding effort was in full swing. Mart poisoned the prisoners, not to kill them, just to control them. The captives were released to work, but had to get a daily antidote for the poison or die horribly. Korin approved, it was simple and elegant. Brig who was dying of poison was less enthused about it.

Korin began to worry about Brig. He looked so thin and gaunt. Korin was unsure what was keeping him upright, he looked as weak as a new born, yet he was not weak at all, mighty still was his strength and power. Oh, what is she going to tell Jillian when they return, how can she faced her in the face of this horrific news. Brigand Sawyer spoke as if he were reading her mind.

"She already knows Korin, I sent her a message saying my goodbyes while my mind was still my own to direct" Brig said.

Korin reacted in an unexpected way, she collapsed and cried her heart out. Even as she cried, it had finally come home, Brig was going to die and be no more. Brig knelt down and scooped up Korin like a child and held her close to him. Brig smelled like the native flower that grew nearby, sweet and robust. His strong arms pinned her to him. Why did she have to find a great love only to loose it again so soon, but then again when was Korin's life ever fair?

On the sixth day at the tenth hour Rok and Bello emerged from the ruined base dragging four raggedy forms with them. Matho walked out of the opening behind them looking exhausted and starving. The four persons who were brought out with the guardians were the top officials from the old government, Rok threw them on the ground and made a sour face and walked away shaking his bald dirty head. Bello was as grime as a man could be. He pointed at the four men and shook with pent up rage. However, it was not Bello who explained, but Matho who was able to find his voice.

"These men gassed their own troops and with a chemical that drove the men insane, then killed them. They did this so that none of the soldier could tell us where they were hiding. They killed thousands to protect their own worthless necks. The look on many of the dead soldiers faces called for mercy or a second chance at life, meaning they did not know they were dying, they did not volunteer to sacrifice themselves, it was thrust upon them" Matho said in a low growl.

Brig thought how much the youth had grown; he was not a boy anymore but a man, who had his childhood stolen from him by the horrors of war, and the atrocities of the men before him.

"I would have killed them on the spot, but you asked me to bring them back to you" Matho said in disgust.

"It falls to Mart and yourself to judge them Matho. He is the new governor I think and you're the law son, so it is up to you to pass sentence on them" Brig said as he looked at the other three Guardians for their input, they only nodded their head that he was correct.

"What say you people of Pirz, what is to be the fate of these four, do we show mercy or do they pay the final bill" Mart asked loudly.

A huge man with grey hair and a big belly walked up and raised his hand to be recognized to speak to the group.

"My son and daughter were taken by the ruling counsel troops and they never came home, I believe them dead. What right do these men have to mercy when they have shown none even to the loyal troops who stood to protect them? I say we hang them from the bridge over the rise there" The big man said pointing to the north.

"Mercy, I don't want to die" Sniveled one of the rulers.

That day the Pirz became a different people, ruled by their own, openly democratic governor Mart. Mart appointed Matho as head of the law givers, this caused a great roar of approval. Matho was a quiet young man, who had learned the difference between justice and revenge. Matho swore to bring in the guilty who broke the law to the court and let the court judge them.

The old ruling counsel were judged, sentenced and hung from the bridge in the valley until they were dead. Their bodies were burnt to ash and tilled into the land so they could give back to the planet they had abused.

The Kyl soldiers and four guardians hung around for a few days to help rebuild the town and government before departing for Kyl?

CHAPTER 13: LAST SACRIFICE

When the drop ship had brought everyone up from Pirz and they had settled in and showered, Milo called the Guard to his Captain's mess for dinner. Korin came in another simple yet slinky frock that made the boys glad they were boys. Rok wore a tee shirt that Brig jacked from Kerra's stash of all things Earth, it said "Bigger and stronger, but cuddly too". Bello was in uniform, as he always was. Brig wore a clean white shirt and white linen slacks, but he went bare foot to the meal. Wherever Brig stepped the floor was searing hot, likely the reason he was shoeless.

"I hate to be a bummer from the start of the meal, but we are in a bad way as far as traveling goes" Milo explained.

"Then let us handle that after we eat Captain; for, we have had a hellova time out here on vacation and I am hungry." Brig said.

"Vacation...oh God's sake!" Rok boomed.

Everyone laughed at the irony of Brig's words and they had a fine meal.

The meal was over and the gathered friends went to the duties and activities that required their personal attention. Bello went to the engine room to see what could be done about the damaged parts. He was not happy when he finally went to his cabin to sleep, because he could see no solution to their problem.

Rok sat on the floor with his big feet on the bed reading a book; it had been too long since he had enjoyed a quiet moment with an engaging story. He was not worried about the trip home, wherever he was at the present was good enough for him. Life as a guardian meant lots of travel and sleeping where you could, if you could. Therefore, if the trip was a long ride home so be it.

Korin was lying on her bed waiting for Brig to come and stay with her. When he did not come, she went to look for him. Brig was in a heated discussion with Milo about something, but they both stopped dead when she arrived. Milo saluted and took his leave.

"Well met little Korin, miss me did you" Brig said?

"Come to bed, and hold me. Have you seen the ships doctor, can they do anything for you" Korin asked hopefully.

"There is nothing they can do" Brig dashed Korin's hopes on the rocks.

"Well stop wasting our time together out here in the halls, come to bed and cuddle me" Korin said all sexy.

"Fine, to bed then" Brig said in an extremely tired voice.

In the pitch black of the night in space, the ship lurched forward so violently that it tossed everything all over. Rok had he not been lying on the floor in his cabin would have hit the wall. Bello was tossed right off his bunk. Korin woke with a start and reached for Brig to make sure that he was okay. Brigand Sawyer was not there, not on the floor, not in the cabin.

There was a general quarters call, and all the crew began to jump to battle stations, even though there did not seem to be any attack. Rather, the damn ship was going like; well, like gang busters.

(Earlier that morning in engineering).

The engine room and engineering teams were meeting to try to figure out how to get the ship into port on Kyl this century, because if they didn't think of something soon, that is how long the trip would take on the smaller jump engines. They must be able to use the Star drive if they were to ever see Kyl in their life time.

"What would it take to get the star drive going boys and girls" A voice in the corridor asked?

"A bloody miracle, the power cuppler is fried mate" the Chief answered. "Step in here and let us see who we are addressing".

   It was a shock when the face that came into the room, belonged to the most dangerous person on the ship, the chief wanted to instantly apologize, but could not get his tongue to work for him. All of the crew pressed up against the walls in fear, they had heard of the insane beating this man had given to the Pirz forces, he had been shot down and refused to die, even now, the wound was there for anyone to see. Brig walked in among them took a deep breath and began his idea on how to get home.

"Can the cuppler be jumped by an insulator of some sort, or spliced" Brig asked/

The chief looked at the crew and turned a sad face to the Guardian.

"Sadly no, sir. I tried that first" the chief explained.

"I don't think you understand my questions chief, so let me say it a different way. If I held one end of the cuppler and grabbed the other end could my power as a guardian sustain the circuit and get this tub home" Brig asked? "Before you answer, know this, I am dying even now and I don't have a damn thing to loose, this may be my last act as Guardian and as a man".

"Brig, your stronger than any man I have ever known, and it is in theory possible, but there is no way to know for sure" Chief told him.

"Then my friend let's do it and find out. One more thing not a word, not a single word of how it was done to anyone, not even Milo. Lie if you have to, make something up, just don't let any of the Guard or Milo see what becomes of me. Please. I just want to

get my friends home as my last act of love." Brig said
sincerely and held out his hand for the chief to shake.

The jump-engines, do just that they get the ship jumping toward
the speed that are required to light off the star drive. The chief
and his crew had the jump engines snarling like hungry tigers,
and they squeezed out all the power they could to keep the
speed up to peak before Brig gave his idea a shot. The chief
wanted to give the plan the best chance possible to succeed,
When the ship was skipping along at a good speed, the chief told
Brig that it was time if he still wanted to do it. Brigand sawyer,
small human male from a little blue marble in space, smiled and
waved to the crew, without any hesitation he grabbed the first
part of the cable cuppler and wrapped it around his forearm and
hand, satisfied that it was secures, he reached out and snapped
the opposite part of the broken cuppler and poured all of his
power from his G-jen into the ships star drive. The flag ship
accelerated so hard the ship nearly came apart. Brig was just
standing there with his eyes closed in a red curtain of power. The
star drive grabbed hold and they jumped into hyperspace. Never,
before had any ship ever endured such speed, the star drive was
using minimal power and they were burning thru the light years
of space in a quarter the normal time.

"My God, he did it, and he is maintaining the circuit even now,
keeping the power output constant. I am not even sure he is still
alive" The chief said.

"What the hell just happened down there, how did we jump to
hyperspace" Milo growled in the com?

The chief had tears in his eyes, and had to steady himself
before answering the captain. He cleared his throat and walked
up to the com unit.

"We overcame the problem and tested our solution to see if were
viable" The chief said.

"You did not even let the bridge know you were testing a new
idea" Milo said in a huff.

"What are you bitching about Milo, we are going like a bat out of hell. It will be days until we reach Kyl instead of months" The chief said in anger.

True to his word the navigator confirmed that the assertion was correct, the ship was moving at impossible speeds and, if they kept it up for another 6 days they would indeed by in Kyl's orbit. Milo was pleased with the engine crew, but how did they do it, when he the former engineering officer was baffled. He went down to the engine room and found the doors welded shut. Milo was once again confused, why would someone weld the door shut?

"Chief this is the captain, why is the engine room's door welded shut" Milo asked into the com.

"The solution was a dangerous one Milo, and we can't risk your life or anyone else to satisfy curiosity, so for safety sake the doors were welded up" The chief answered.

The captain of the ship decided that the chief was likely right, it was best to keep the door closed if the tech used was of a dangerous nature; he had a ship and crew to get home after all. If he had known what was behind that door, he would have had kittens.

The three Guardians looked everywhere for Brig, to no avail though, they could not find him. Korin tried the com, her psychic link with Brig and nothing happened. Bello told Rok he could sense Brig's power and the G-jen were still on the ship and active, it was just he did not know whereto look. Rok questioned all the crew and searched the ship, he did not find Brig. Korin was beside herself; she went to Milo and said she could not find Brig and as everyone knew Brig is ill. She asked Milo to help find Brig, and he said it would be his top priority.

On the sixth day in hyperspace Milo took Rok to the last place on the ship that had not been searched, the engine room. Rok ripped the door off the hinges and fell to his knees when he looked in the door. Rok cried, so did Milo. Rok's wail of anguish reverberated through the entire ship.

"What the hell was that" Korin said?

"That is Ultimate suffering Korin" Bello said flatly, he knew they had found Brig and he feared Korin's actions.

The two guardians ran down to the ships engine room. Milo was there choking the life out of the old chief, Rok was against the wall still wailing in grief. Bello went to stop Milo from killing the chief when he stopped and almost had a heart attack and died on the spot.

"What have you done" Screamed Milo "How could you do this to him".

Korin grabbed Milo by the back of the neck and tossed him on top of Rok. She walked up to where Brig was floating in the red energy that came from within him, and out through his G-jen. She turned to Milo and spoke in a calm voice.

"All of us put together could not force that man to do anything, Milo. It is not the chief's fault. Don't you see; Brig was dying and this was the last selfless heroic thing he could do for all of us? He wanted to just get us home. He made the chief keep his mouth shut because we would have tried to stop him from doing this" Korin said in a soft whispered.

Brigs hands up to his wrist were burnt and the skin was breaking down, Brig was not dead yet, how he lived was beyond Bello's knowledge. Why couldn't it have been him, instead of Brigand? Brig was worth a hundred Bello's the guardian thought. He spoke with passion and then paid the price for that conviction with his own blood and body. Hero, was to skinny of a term for this man. Bello was joined by Milo and Rok, all who sat against the wall in the engine room paying silent tribute to the hero of the mission. A scream of such magnitude shook the ship and rent a comet to nothingness.

"I was wrong before, that is the sound of the deepest anguish imaginable; it is the sound of Korin's heart burning in her chest. It is the sound of the galaxy crying for Brigand Sawyer's soul, so profound is this loss that the universe has changed." Bello said honestly.

The look on Jar face when he came on board of the flag ship, was shock and disbelief. Jar tried to remove Brig from the machine and was nearly killed for his efforts. Milo tried to explain the situation to Jar, but the arrogant Guardian leader was not listening. Korin lost her temper and punched Jar in the face then threw him like a Frisbee out of the ships hatch. Kerra came in, the sight of Brig's burnt hand and used up body, made her break down, she began to wail. Rok picked her up and carried her away. The chief told them somehow Brig had infused the system with his spirit, and the ship refuses to shut down, much the same as Brig himself. He told them he was not sure how to remove his hero. He never had to find a way; the task was taken from his hands.

"Everyone get the hell out." Jillian said pulling her Glave bladed sword from her muscular back.

The crew and the chief left as Oru pushed them out of the way and then blocked the door.

"No, I mean get off the damned ship!" Jillian yelled in anger!

The ship was empty, and Jillian stood there looking at the boy she fell in love with as a little girl, the hero of her life and the prince of all her dreams. Jillian never wanted anyone else, just Brig. She never considered life without him until now. Oru was keening in the corner, huge tear ran on to the metal floor, but the mighty Oru made almost no sound out of respect for Jillian's feelings. Oru and Jillian had become bonded and close, they were BFF as the saying goes. Jillian could feel the pain in her friend, like Korin, Oru was not good at getting close to people, and loosing one was worse for him than the genial Jillian.

"Come Oru lets get our Brig out of this can and take him home"

Jillian said.

In a flash of her deadly techno-magi blade Brigand Sawyer dropped into the Wira's waiting arms. Brig was warm to the touch, but he did not breathe. He was dead. Oru carried Brig out of the ship, and thousands of Kylr lined up and paid respect to the fallen hero. An ocean of tears ran in the streets as Oru made his way to the crystal chapel were all Guardians were celebrated and mourned after their passing. When they arrive Bello, Rok, Milo and Elon were there waiting for them. Jillian had met the huge Grot before and knew him to be a kind and generous being.

"Ms Jillian I have a request. Since the hero Brigand Sawyer lost his life in service to my planet, I ask on the behalf of my father the king and my own humble self that we be allowed to burry Brig on Grot as a hero to our world" Elon said Gently?

"It is the greatest honor that he offers Brig Jillian" Said Jamis.

The speaker of the Kylr people looked at Brig in Oru's arms with a strange look on his face, almost happy, or perhaps surprise. Maybe it was just respect, Jillian was upset and could not tell. She took a deep breath and addressed everyone gathered.

"It is my wish, that Brig be buried on Grot as a hero, and it is my demand that his own reverend Mike Goode preside over the service. He will have to be fetched from Earth immediately. Lastly, Brig is to be buried with his G-jen in place, if anyone tries to remove it; I will kill them" Jillian said with her eyes blazing. Oru roared like a loin scaring everyone except Korin.

"I will see to the arrangements, Kerra will go to Earth for the holy man in my own ship" Jamis said bluntly.

Korin was about to blow, her heart was broken, but not her spirit.

"One final thing, Grot prince, if you or anyone on Grot so much as licks Brig's hand I will turn Grot to ash" Korin said with insane conviction.

"I accept your warning and welcome it if we sin against our hero Brigand Sawyer. I am of great honor Korin of the green eyes, I would rather die than live with shame" Elon said, and his word was law on Grot, even the King did not cross him.

CHAPTER 14: BURIAL

It was Sunday and the Rev. Mike Goode was finishing his sermon for the morning. The congregation was all awake and bright eyed. The spirit of the Lord was glowing today, and Mike was on fire. It was one of the most inspiring speeches he had ever given. As the church let out for the day, Mike went to his office to look over his afternoon schedule. Little did the man know he was about to take a journey of a life time.

When the door the his office opened Mike did not even look up, thinking it was just his wife or one of the elders coming in for a book or reference materials. The door closed and there was silence. Complete silence, there were even no birds chirping or cars on the road leaving the church, there was just plain nothing. Mike looked up and was startled. Before his were a tall blue man with a bald head and slate grey- blue eyes, very fit in a white uniform of some sort. Beside him was the most beautiful woman he had ever seen, Next to his own wife that is. She was in a white sheer gown that went to her knees and she was smiling at Mike in a suggestive way.

"Can I help you" Mike asked pleasantly?

"Are you Rev. Mike Goode" The blue man asked in a flat serious voice?

"Yes I am" Mike said.

"We have come to get you for a funeral, you are to say words over the lost hero, it was Jillian's wish" the blue girl said.

"Listen young woman, I am a busy man, I have a great many responsibilities to attend to, I can't just pick up and leave" Mike said gently.

(Laughter)

"My good man, I am 97 of your years old, and you will come because you must. I am afraid one of your own people has died, one Brigand Sawyer. He died far away from your little planet and his mate Jillian Robins requires you to say the holy words of your book over Brig. So you are coming sir, and I am not asking you. I am Kerra chief medical counsel of the Kylr and grand counsel member, this buff soul is my mate Jar leader of all the Kyl guardians, the universal police force if you will, Brig was recruited by us and served better than any one before him ever has. His loss was devastating to us all, as you will see." Kerra explained.

"Sir time is short and we have a long way to go, to reach Grot where the funeral will be held, please ready yourself." Jar said sternly. Jar did not want to be here.

"It will take time, there are arrangement to be made, I can't just..."Mike was explaining.

One minute Mike was at his desk thee next moment he was sitting in a seat aboard Jamis's private ship, being strapped in by Jar. Who gave him a hard look to stop any argument forth-coming. Kidnapped was what just happened to the pastor from a small church in Washington state. Mike decided since he had no choice he might as well learn to enjoy the wonders he was likely to see out here in space. How many men will ever get to see what I am about to? Mike sat back and looked out the port side window as the moon swept by, then Jupiter and so on.

"Kyl is far away Mike, it is a paradise. Our technology is life times ahead of Earth's, our people do not know disease, poverty, famine, or ignorance. However, with every boon comes a challenge. We have a very low birth rate, so we plan to mix with our Earth friends and raise up both races to a stronger bond, what are your thoughts holy man?" Kerra said playfully.

"I am not sure how to answer; except we are all God's children."

Mike said honestly.

"Our society is very different from Earths, we don't take a permanent mate, do to the birth issue, we pair up with whom ever can help us achieve a baby. This is a practice you would likely not approve of. Even though in you holy book, it says to be fruitful and multiply. "Kerra answered.

"I am not here to pass judgments, I was brought to lay a friend to rest, so I think it best that I focus on that to the exclusion of all else." Mike said.

"Jillian said you are a wise man; and so you are sir." Kerra said.

The vastness of the galaxy and then the broader universe never ceased to amaze Mike. When he had seen what he thought was the most interesting sight ever, the next instant something even more breath taking would appear and he would be floored again. Yes, I am a lucky man to be able to see all of this.

One day after Mike was kidnapped, the ship arrived on Kyl. When Pastor Mike got off the ship and he looked around at the architecture and general splendor of it all. It was just like Kerra had said, it truly was a paradise. Every person young or old, all of which it was impossible to tell their ages, were all gorgeous and fit. The air was sweat and pollution free, the sun was crisp and playful. Mike felt like a child who just got out of school for the summer. A Handsome older Kylr came to Mike and held out a hand to shake. Mike shook his hand vigorously.

"I am Jamis, speaker for the Kylr people and Kerra's fathe.r" Jamis said. "My apologies for the abduction and abrupt way we have acted, it is for a just cause I assure you. Do you remember Brigand Sawyer Reverend"?

"Yes, I do know him. He was a strange boy, small and shy, that is until something set him off. It was usually in Jillian's defense, and then he was a wild cat. It was baffling to see the transformation from one spectrum to the other" Mike said.

"Yes, Brig was a passionate young man, he gave it all for the greater good, the last time was the last time" Jamis said sadly. "We need to prepare you and get on our way to Grot quickly, and then we can return you home sir with our profound thanks".

The trip to Grot was one of great instruction. Jamis educated Mike on the politics of the universe and what races were more likely to kill you for the sport of it. He told Mike several time to never be parted with the Guardians for any reason, they were his only protection. Mike listened and learned at a fevers pace. Kerra stayed away form Mike because her near nudity seemed to bother him, and since he was a holy man she did not think flirting with him was indicated, not even for fun. Jar kept his distance as well, Mike did not know why. Kerra later told him that Jar didn't believe in God, but he was a fool for it. Kerra told Mike that the maker was the reason the universe it so lovely, why when you love someone it is so special, especially when your apart. Mike decided that Kerra was much more than she seemed. Jamis told him that Kerra was a genius, her mind was beyond most geniuses as well, her IQ was immeasurable

Grot was a more wild planet, meaning more untamed territory and wilderness. You could see wild game roaming around the edge of the landing platform, they moved off when the ship came in for a touch down. Jamis was greeted by a monster, it was 10' and 600-800lbs. The behemoth had a scaly armor plating all over, four finger hands and car crusher arms. It turned it's giant hazel eyes on Mike. Jamis told Mike earlier that the Grot were omnivores and they eat everything, from animals to enemies, so Mike was scared.

"Greetings Rev. Mike Goode, it is very nice to meet you even in these sad times" Elon said softly.

"Thank you" Mike said in a shaky voice.

Elon just smiled, he knew to a race such as Earthling, who were isolated from the great races in the universe he must seem a great big nightmare, and, well he was. Not this day however, today he was here to meet this man and escort him the monument he had built for Brig. Elon took a floating cargo looking sled and encourage everyone to get aboard. The trip to the grave sight took only a few minute on the fast gravity defying sled, but country side was awe inspiring.

The gathered crowd parted at the approach of Elon, some out of respect, most out of fright at the giant size and power. Jillian was standing beside the crystal structure looking at Mike. He did not know it was her, the change in the once model was complete. She was more beautiful now than she had ever been. Jillian had a wild strength about her now, and down her back hung a sword. Her blue eyes burned with an inner fire that was frightening to look into. Jillian was different, she no longer looked to need a champion, she was her own. Beside her was a slender blue girl with snake like green eyes in a short silver mini dress, she was as beautiful as Jillian and built physically that same Jillian, only her breasts were smaller. The girl wore a gauntlet on her arm like Jar did and she had red rimmed eyes from the million tears that they had shed. Both Jillian and the Blue girl were bare foot and holding hands. Mike stepped forward and was stopped by a blue giant.

"Hello, I am Mike Goode and your are" Mike said

"Rok".

"Let him pass little brother" The blue goddess said softly.

The giant moved aside and when Mike passed, he fell in behind him as they walked up to where Jillian stood. Jillian's eyes were haunted and distant as if she were the one who died. Jillian placed her open hand on Mike's shoulder and smiled with out any joy.

"Thank you for coming Pastor Mike, Brig would want only you to be the one to commit his soul to God's open hands. He always respected you and your way. I had you brought here as a tribute to my Brigand" Jillian said

"I am Korin, it is a pleasure to meet any of Brig's friends" Korin said.

Mike thought what a frail girl she was, Jillian must be protection and shielding her from these powerful aliens. Later, Jamis would fully explained Korin to Mike, and how dangerous that girl really was. Mike was shocked at the list of deeds Korin had amassed. Rok was her partner in the last campaign along with Brig and Bello. There was so many things that seemed out of place here to Mike, were sense was lost to the reality of the moment.

"I would say it is a pleasure Ms. Korin; but I was brought here to burry a friend" Mike said.

The crystal item Jillian's hand was resting on was not for show. Within it was Brigand Sawyer's body. Brig was battle wore and his hands were a burnt mess. His face however, was the picture of peacefulness. If Mike did not know better he would have thought that Brig was happily sleeping. Upon Brig's left arm was a golden gauntlet with a giant red gem, a ruby perhaps. Mike looked at Korin and her G-jen was also golden, Rok and Bello sported a silver one. Mike wondered what the difference was, if there even was one. Mike found it odd that this lovely alien girl would be more broken up about Brig's death than Jillian who he loved him all her life. Once again Mike was mistaken. Jillian was holding back all her emotions, like Moses did the red sea. Jillian needed to follow through for Brigand's sake without breaking down and loosing herself to despair. Korin just could not hold her crushed heart back, her story would explain her reaction to loosing the only man who ever loved her. Something else Mike would be told later. The Earth Pastor turned to the crowd and spoke.

"Let us assemble and send our friend off properly" Mike stated

Korin snapped her fingers and Rok herded the crowd where they needed to be for the service. Jillian just held Korin's hand and touch the final resting place of her lover and life companion. On the opposite side of the Crystal case was a field set up like an amphitheatre, all the various races began to find seats, some stood off to the side, and the Pirz ambassador was one of those. He seemed happy to attend Brig's funeral.

"Friends and gathered family, we are here today to remember Brigand Sawyer. He was born on a small farm in Washington State, well, back on our planet. I baptized him. I married his parent and the parents of his long time girlfriend Jillian Robins. I never thought to be at his funeral, but I am not all that surprised. I would like to tell you a story that illustrates the character of this young man. When Brigand was about fourteen he came upon a 3 year old girl who was crying in front of a burning barn. Brig called the fire dept and then looked after the girl. The child told him her kitty was in the burning barn, without a second thought Brig kicked the door in and ran inside, he found the little animal and gave it to the child. Brig was already barfing up smoke. The child said her doll, the one her mother gave her before she died was in the barn as well, and she would die of a broken heart if she lost it. Brig got up off the ground and jumped passed the fireman who was trying to put out the raging inferno; he went back into the death trap after a doll because it meant everything for the child. Brig's back and legs were burned; he protected the doll with his body so the child could have it back in one piece. It took three firemen to hold him down and get an oxygen mask on him and dress his burns. Brig was never a large person, and he was never aggressive or mean. However, I have never known anyone with more fight in him than Brigand Sawyer. When his parents died he took care of everything, he was seventeen. When his neighbor, and old man could not get out when it snowed Brig took him food and chopped all of his wood for him, then stacked it by his porch so he could stay warm. Brigand Sawyer has always been a hero to me, strong and true, willing to sacrifice himself for a friend or family. It appears that he gave his life, just as his lived, being a true hero and a solid man. I notice that Brigand still wears the stainless steel cross that I gave him as a small boy; it is around his neck even now. Brigand never wronged anyone and tried to live his life as his God would have wanted. Therefore, I commend the soul and body of Brigand Sawyer a true hero to the embrace of our Lord God" Pastor Mike Goode stated is a clear upbeat tone, with just a hint of emotion shoving through.

There were very few dry eyes in the crowds of thousands who came to send Brig off. The Grot stood as one and pounded their massive chests in harmony. All of the Kyl Guardians turned their G-jen toward the sky and the combine blast set a rainbow of color across the violet sky. Oru the Wira sang a song that made the strongest among the crowd weep like a new born babe. Rok and Elon picked up the crystal case holding Brig and set it on a lift that would put it deep into the ground.

"Goodbye my brother, I hope to make you proud of me" Rok choked out.

"May you find prey to hunt and joy in you eternity" Elon added.

One by one the thousands of Kylr, Grot and a few Pirz such as Matho and Mart paid their friend a fond farewell. Matho, who was usually very stoic, cried unashamed. When the many had come and placed a hand on the crystal and made a wish for peace to Brig, then his closest friends and family came.

"Had I a son Brigand Sawyer, I would have wished him to be as you are, a leader, a man and a great friend, loyal and true. It shames me that with all our knowledge we could not save you" Jamis said with tears on his cheeks.

"I had thought I knew more about science and medicine than any other person in the universe. I have grown complacent in my arrogance, I vow I will not let another die from the venom of those damn snakes; I will hunt with Jillian and capture one to study. I will discover the cure and treatment Brigand Sawyer. One more thing before I go, I carry the child of yours and Jillian's seed, I ask for your forgiveness for stealing what was not mine to take" Kerra said emotionally.

Kerra and Jamis moved away and Jar approached the crystal to a hostile look from Korin. Jar did not miss it and he tried to suppress the instant shutter of fear that passed through him; he failed.

"You are the new bench mark that all the Guard must now aspire to" Jar said.

"It is from you that we the Guardians of the Kylr and the universe re-learned the meaning of duty and honor and service and (Bello shook and tried not to cry, but he lost the battle) SACRICIE" Bello managed before he fell to pieces, which for a man of complete control was hard to take. Brig had made him feel relevant again, proud to be a Guardian, that stood for something more important that just themselves.

Korin and Jillian walked up to the crystal hand in hand. Korin crawled up and laid on top of Brig's crystal coffin, she cried softly and mashed her face into the crease where Brig's face was as if she were trying to crawl in with him. Jillian put her head on Korin's back and spoke to soft for anyone to hear, Korin only shook her head a little to show that she had heard. No one went near them, nobody moved, they just waited the hour or so that the girls stayed there unmoving. Jillian stood up and finally addressed the gathered assembly.

"Here rests the best man who ever lived, my heart and soul, my strength and my protector. If anyone or anything disturbs Brig's final rest there will be no place in the universe we wont track you down and my make you pray for death" Jillian said with enough poison in her voice to make even Elon shudder.

"I would not echo the words of Jillian, I have no mercy in me, you know this for a fact, what little restraint I may have shown has died with Brigand Sawyer. Ware the reaper once more" Korin said as green lightning snapped out and around her and Jillian.

Wild were the hearts of these two goddesses, and vengeful are their souls. Jar and Jamis both looked ill at the repercussions of these two girls. Nothing short of death could stop them. Here rests Brigand Sawyer the most fierce fighter Jar had ever known and in his place were not one but two replacements, with less mercy. Despair was soon to follow no doubt.

They placed Brigand in a specially lined tome, that was immune to the elements and grave robbers. The Grot set an eternal flame to burning over the tome and a guard who would stand post 24 hours a day forever. The girls thought this a special honor and they told Elon that he was going to have a special place in their hearts for this act of honor. He only bowed low and properly as a response.

Brigand Sawyer born Dec 21 1982, died Nov 11 2012 on an alien planet. Brig found himself buried on Grot, in the wilds where his spirit belonged.

Pastor Mike was transported by Rok, back to Earth and he was given a singular honor, Rok gave him a com and told him if the need ever arose where he needed the services of a guardian for any reason, Rok would come no questions asked to his aid. Pastor Mike was indeed honored, however he never used the com. Sadly Pastor Mike would pass into the veil late the next year from an undisclosed medical condition. Mike was a great man and his loss was felt by thousands of people, who in his life Mike had touched and enriched, not only though the word of God, but from his own golden soul.

CHAPTER 15: AFTERMATH.

In the months after Brig was put to rest, Korin and Jillian stayed together and leaned on each other for support. Oru came and went, his powerful heart broken. Oru knew the reason Brig was in the grave was that he gave his life so that Oru may live. More and more Oru was staying away for longer periods of time, until one day he just did not return at all.

Jillian knew it was only a matter of time before Korin left as well. No matter how much Jillian and Korin truly loved each other, it could not fill the void that was there, left by the loss of Brig. It was a black hole. Jillian finally knew the day had come to let Korin go when she woke up and Korin was lying beside her holding her so tight it was hard to breath. Jillian kissed her softly and gave her the last speech she would ever get to say.

"I love you Korin and I set you free. Your not happy here, you heart and spirit need to return to the stars, to your duty, the calling of a hero. You should admit that to yourself and take an assignment and go" Jillian said softly.

"I don't want to leave you Jillian, I love you too. I just can't stay still anymore, I have so much rage in me that I have to do something or I will die. I don't want to leave you alone either, but where I am going you might die and I could not bare that." Korin said with tiny pearls on the rims of her lovely slanted green eyes.

"Then it is settled, I will go with you to the academy and you will seek an assignment and return to the Guardians, take your place as their best and brightest and show the younger and older ones what valor really is." Jillian said as she to cried breathlessly.

The two most beautiful girls on Kyl walked into the academy, now called the Sawyer Guardian Academy after Brigand Sawyer. Korin gave an order to a junior Guard and he just stood there. Korin would have back handed him but Rok's booming voice could be heard coming down the hall.

"Move your ass rookie" Rok hollered! "Do you not know who she is"?

The hapless recruit just stood there stupid. Korin bent forward and kissed him on the lips and whispered her name. The rookie was shaking in fear the instant she finished pronouncing it. Rok was mad at the lack of discipline, but held his tongue.

"I am here to take an assignment little brother" Korin said cheerfully.

"Jar thought you retired and gave me your post as deputy commander of the Guard" Rok explained.

"Hardly, I am never going to retire, and I will die on the job like..." Korin began to say but stopped. I will not stop serving."

Jar was indeed shocked at the appearance of Korin, but Jamis was not. Jamis smiled at the girls and bowed slightly. Jar grim as usual made no move to greet either of them. Jillian still did not know Kerra was pregnant with her child yet, and he feared for Kerra when she found out. Kerra explained what she had done to the counsel earlier, but Jillian was scared and confused at the time and forgot about it. Jamis knew, but would not tell, because he felt it the duty of his daughter and her mate to explain themselves to Jillian. The baby would have three sets of mingled DNA, Brig's, Jillian's and Kerra's. The baby would be a super infant when it was born.

"What brings you here ladies" Jamis asked.

"It is time I went back to work, so much so I am taking command of the entire Guard" Korin said with an edge that asked for a conflict.

Jar eyed her menacingly for a moment but offered her no contestation. Good thing to, Korin would have beaten him to death right there and then. Jamis looked at Korin and smiled.

"A splendid idea, and timely as well, I was about to appoint
Jar to the ambassador spot on Grot. More, Korin you're a natural
leader, next to Brig you the most powerful Guardian in the corps.
When I place the G-jen on your arm, it was not random, I gave
you one of three golden G-jen, and they are by far the most
powerful. One you wear now, one Brig still wears and the other,
well it is hidden for a good reason" Jamis said

"I was not aware that there was a difference in the G-jen, only in
the wearer. If the Guardian is a powerful person, with a great
spirit then they are very powerful, if they have a weak spirit then
they are less powerful" Jar asked.

"True, completely true, however there are three G-jen that do not
fit that rule" Jamis said.

"How dare you give that abomination a golden one, she is unfit to
wear any G-jen" Jar snarled at Jamis.

"Idiot, Korin would be more powerful than any of you no matter
what G-jen she wore, she has never even tapped the special
abilities of her Gauntlet yet, so far her ability is all her will power,
HER will power not the G-jen. I am excepting Korin as supreme
commander of the Guard effective this moment. Do you have
anything you want to say Jar" Jamis said as he narrowed his
eyes.

   Jar was angry not stupid. Jamis had a hidden power that
rivaled any Guardian and he was also the master who taught all
of the original guard to fight, so Jamis was not someone to cross
swords with foolishly, especially with that quick tempered Korin
beside him. Jar would be dead before he could even move
against either of them. Then there was Jillian and her cursed
blade. How had Jar lost control of his life?

"No, I accept the ambassador appointment, it is time for a
change" Jar said as he spun on a heel and left.

"He is so pissed off right now" Jillian said as she let her Glave
blade fall softly point down to the floor, where she leaned on it.

"If he moved you were going to kill him." Jamis asked Jillian surprised?

Jillian smiled a sweat smile and in a deft move sheathed her weapon.

"You are both dear to me, if your life is endangered, than I will defend you if I am able" Jillian explained.

My God the transformation was complete, if Brig could only have lived to see it. Jillian removed her sword from her back and none of them noticed. She had surpassed even Jamis in mastery of the weapon. It both encouraged him and frightened him, because she was so fluid, there would be no defense if she attacked. Her skills were on par with a guardian, and her power with the Glade in her hand was only limited to her spirit. Jillian Robin's spirit was a pulsar burning in her breasts.

Later Jamis would sit in his favorite chair and he would worry about the future. His thoughts were calm about Jillian and Korin who would forge their own way ahead, their destinies were bright, though likely fraught with peril. No, Jamis was worried about Kerra and Earth and the bursting conflict brewing out there. More, what was the strange ship cloaked over Grot? Who was it, and why cloak over Grot? My God of all the times to need a hero now was it, and Brig when I really need you, your lying in a grave.

EPILOG

In the wilderness of the planet Grot there is this day a trail of blood leading deeper into the frontier. There is an alien with long matted hair walking in a torn and bloody rag that was once a uniform. His steps were erratic and measured because he wobbled and nearly fell with each one he took. His stomach growled and sent a wave of nausea to his already light head. It was not just hunger but a terrible burning thirst.

Tarocs were grazing a mile or so away from the alien who was steadily moving their way. Tarocs are a four horned herd animal. They have two horns that jut out below their lower jaw and two that extend just above their big round red eyes. A Taroc weighs around two thousand pounds; they are hunted for food by the Grot. Tarocs are therefore skittish about strangers or anything that is not one of them. At present the herd was drinking water and eating the wild fruit near the water to fatten up for the herd movement to the east, where they would mate.

The alien walked right up to a huge Taroc and looked at it. If the animal could eat the fruit it was not poison he thought to himself, then again I am not one of them. What if this is not my world and I crashed here? Oh the hell with it, the alien's stomach lurched and the alien convulsed with pain at not having had any food in it way to long. The alien decide to chance it, starvation was not a way to die. The fruit was juicy and delicious; the juice ran down the alien's face and on to his chest. The alien reached up and scratched the Taroc right between its eyes. The normally skittish animal just closed its eyes and enjoyed the scratch and even grunted its pleasure. Side by side the animal and the alien enjoy a meal, the then the Taroc led the alien down to the water to drink and wash the juices off their faces.

As the day waned the alien followed his new Taroc friend to the east away from the Grot city some twenty six miles away. At night the alien saw the lights but it bought no interest to him.

(Elsewhere on Grot)

    Elon was in chambers with his father the king about the growing unrest in the galaxy and the requests by many planets to aid them if war broke out. One major problem was that both side wanted them as allies. Therefore that was the main subject of their conversation. The king being wise knew Elon to be a better expert on the Non-Grot worlds and the races that lived there. He would have the prince decide who the Grot would back. Elon would no doubt pick the winning side and stay out of harms way. The guardians were closer to the Grot than they had been in years, so they would side with the Grot as well. Being the King of the Grot was a good deal right now.

"Excuse the interruption your kinglyness" Said a big brute of a Grot Page.

"Yes".

"Pardon the bad news, but I was directed to come and tell you immediately if any news ever involved the tome of Brig the hero" The Page said.

"Well, what is the news" Elon asked?

    The page began to shake with fear of the retribution of the mad prince when he explained the nature of the news. The prince noticed he was stalling and stamped his massive foot to get the pages attention.

"Sorry, but the tome has been ripped open and the body of the hero is gone" the page said.

"Oh MY GOD. Then we are at war with the Kylr. Spread the news, we are at a state of alert until I countermand that order" Elon yelled. "I will go get Jar and we will look at the tome together".

Jar was shaken at the news; he silently followed Elon to the tome. They saw the tome ripped apart and the crystal coffin was shattered and lay in fragments all over the place. It was blasted apart, no missing that, both of them are experience warriors, so they saw that right away... The thing that threw them was the blood leading not to the port and ships, but out toward the frontier and the waste lands

MY BOOK COLLECTION:

VAMPIRE HERO SERIES;
BLOOD BY DAY
SHADOW'S REVENGE
SHADOW GUARD

GUARDIAN SERIES:
ENTER THE GUARDIANS: KYL
LOST ON GROT

THE ASHAN CHRONICALS:
BLACK WINGS

THE ELEMENTAL KIDS SERIES: (kids –young adult)
WORLD OF ICE
WAR FOR ICE

THE DRAGON AND FIRE SERIES (PG)
BREATH OF MAGIK

RYAN THE WILDFIRE/ ALBERT YETI: (young adults)
RYAN OF THE WILDFIRE

ADULT VAMPIRE SERIES: (Adult)
VAMPIRE WARS: BEGINNING

THE LORDS OF ORDER SERIES: (PG)
DESTINY'S KEY

LITTLE MONSTERS (Kids) book one
THE SPRITE ADVENTURE BOOK 2 RONAN'S BOOK
GAVIN THE GNOME BOOK 3

COWARD SERIES:
TAD'S TALE

AN ASSASSIN'S TALE

ONE DARK NIGHT (VAMPIRES) EROTIC

A VILLAIN STORY?
HERO'S BLOOD

HIDDEN

LIST OF TERMS AND PEOPLE:

Earth: planet, home to human race

Kyl: planet gigantic, home to the Kylr, guardians of the universe

Grot: Planet mid sized, home of the war like Grot

Pirz: planet, 4 moons, home of the Pirz

Brigand Sawyer: Human, 5'7 150lbs, light brown hair, red-brown eyes, lover of Jillian and Korin, only non-Kylr Guardian

Jillian Robins: Human, 5'9, 110lbs, red-brown hair, blue eyes, ex model, Lover of Brig and Korin

Korin: Kylr, female, 5'7, 115lbs, silver hair, green snake eyes, only female Guardian, lover of Brig and Jillian

Rok: Kylr, guardian 7'5, 400lbs giant, Blue skin, slate blue grey eyes, bald like all Kylr males, part of the terrible trio with Korin, and Brig, unstoppable together.

Bello: Kylr Guardian, 6', 185, Blue skin adopted brother of Brig, elegant and deadly

Jar: commander of all the Guardians, Blue, 200lbs, 6', Kerra's lover

Kerra: Kylr genius medical Dr, counsel member, Jamis daughter, Jar's mate, nympho, hottest of all Kylr females

Milo: Kylr flag ship captain, young

Jamis: Kylr elder, speaker for all the Kyl, first Guardian, Kerra's dad, the man who beat the Grot invaders, and kept the peace afterwards, master of all Kyl martial weapons, ultra powerful.

Kylr: blue skinned, genetically perfect people, all pretty and fit, cant have babies often, guardians of the universe, Men are bald, women have white silver hair, they are hedonistic people, very sexy because of baby shortage, and they need Earth to save them.

Grot: big scale armored meat eating warrior race, 7'+, 500lbs+, mean, hungry, honorable, combat is everything to them.

Elor: Grot male 1rst commander of Grot forces, later prince and then king, Jamis friend.

Elor 3: Grandsons of Grot king Elor, current king of the Grot, mean

Elon; Grot Prince, best fighter the Grot have ever had 10', 600lbs, elegant statesman, reasonable, Jamis close friend.

Pirz: green-ish skin, all shapes and sizes, war like

Mart: rebel leader of the Pirz common people

Matho: a kids who leaner to fight and kill from the Kyl Guardians

ORU: Wira Monkey, Lasomorph (shape changer) he is

Brig's BFF; they are bonded in the soul to each other, friend of Jillian and Korin, Extremely Powerful, and unconditional loyalty.

ABOUT THE AUTHOR:

Shane was born Dec 21st, in Portland Oregon, to his mother Toffy Lee Wilson and Oscar Joel Wilson. He has an older sister Cookie Caroline Sinclair and a younger brother Curtis Casey Wilson.

Shane currently lives in Vancouver Washington with his Wife of over twenty years, Arlene; and he son Joston and his daughter Jessica Lee.

Shane races Quads and has won 13 over all championships. Joston has won two and Jessica has one title to her credit as well.

Shane has studied Martial arts for nearly thirty years and has a 5th degree black belt in KAJUKENBO.

Shane loves to entertain people with his stories; so her beautiful wife bought him a laptop and told him to put them all to paper. It is Shane's goal to write 100+ books and publish them all. At his current rate; he will reach his goal in under ten years time.

Shane offers this bit of advice:

"IF YOU THINK YOU CAN; THEN YOU ARE RIGHT. IF YOU THINK YOU CAN'T THEN YOU ARE ALSO RIGHT. THEREFORE, NEVER LET ANYTHING BEAT YOU!"

MY PERSON MANTRA IS:

I CAN'T BE BEAT; BECAUSE I WONT BE BEAT.

I MAY NOT ALWAYS WIN, BUT I NEVER LOOSE.

GOD BLESS YOU AND I LOVE YOU.

www.ingramcontent.com/pod-product-compliance
Lightning Source LLC
Chambersburg PA
CBHW021010180626
46814CB00003B/1224